I0743999

COSCOM
ENTERTAINMENT

Also by A.P. Fuchs

Undead World Trilogy

Blood of the Dead
Possession of the Dead
Redemption of the Dead

The Axiom-man™ Saga

Axiom-man or Axiom-man: Tenth year Anniversary Special Edition
First Night Out
Doorway of Darkness
The Dead Land
City of Ruin
Underground Crusade
Outlaw
Rumblings
Frozen Storm (side adventure)
Of Magic and Men (comic book)

Mech Apocalypse

Mech Apocalypse

Other Fiction

A Stranger Dead
A Red Dark Night
April (writing as Peter Fox)
Magic Man (deluxe chapbook)
The Way of the Fog (The Ark of Light Vol. 1)
Devil's Playground (with Keith Gouveia)
On Hell's Wings (with Keith Gouveia)
Zombie Fight Night: Battles of the Dead
Magic Man Plus 15 Tales of Terror
Undeniable
Blood of my World
The Dance of Mervo and Father Clown
Flash Attack: Thrilling Stories of Terror, Adventure, and Intrigue
Giganti-gator Death Machine: Triple Feature

Anthologies (as editor)

Dead Science
Elements of the Fantastic
Vicious Verses and Reanimated Rhymes: Zany Zombie Poetry for
the Undead Head
Metahumans vs the Undead
Bigfoot Terror Tales Vol. 1 (with Eric S. Brown)
Bigfoot Terror Tales Vol. 2 (with Eric S. Brown)
Metahumans vs Werewolves

Non-fiction

Book Marketing for the Financially-challenged Author
Canadian Scribbler: Collected Letters of an Underground Writer
Look, Up on the Screen! The Big Book of Superhero Movie
Reviews
Getting Down and Digital: How to Self-publish Your Book
The Canister X Transmission: Year One
The Canister X Transmission: Year Two
The Canister X Transmission: Year Three
The Canister X Transmission: Year Four
The Canister X Transmission: The Long Year Five

Poetry

The Hand I've Been Dealt
Haunted Melodies and Other Dark Poems
Still About A Girl

www.canisterx.com

It lurked beneath the water, an eye kept toward the surface for anything it could drag under.

Anything made of flesh.

Anything with blood.

Some say they saw it with their own eyes. Others chocked it up as a myth, the stuff of tabloid fiction.

But it was real.

And it was hungry.

GIGANTI-GATOR DEATH MACHINE

TRIPLE FEATURE

by

A.P. Fuchs

COSCOM ENTERTAINMENT
WINNIPEG

ISBN 978-1-927339-73-2

Published by Coscom Entertainment

Text set in Garamond
Printed and bound in the USA

Cover by A.P. Fuchs

For Eric S. Brown.

Table of Contents

Giganti-gator Death Machine

I

PROLOGUE

"I'd stay out of the water if I were you," Yum Yum said.

Chase tried to ignore the old man, but he always had difficulty with that. When Trev "Yum Yum" Goldie said something, you listened. It was his grandpa's raspy voice with the undertone of badass that did it. Yum Yum had been around, especially around these waters here in the South.

"You can't catch any catfish unless you're in the water," Chase said.

"You want to noodle for them things you gotta do it where there's no gator bait all over the place. Told you that already."

"Beats sitting in a boat waitin' on a line."

There were quite a few trees here, most of them growing out of the water, some along the bank, which was a short fifty-foot swim away. Beneath the water were trees that had died and rotted and broke off, and eventually got so water-logged they sank. All sorts of nooks and wooden crannies were under the water; perfect places for catfish to hide.

Noodling for the fish was straight forward: walk around in the waist-deep water, using your feet to feel out what was underneath. Come across places where there were crevasses and insets in the underwater trunks and branches then reach down and hope a catfish was hiding there. The fish would then go for your fingers, and once it clamped on, you gripped its mouth and pulled it out of the water.

Easy fishing.

"Not kidding, Chase. Get back in the boat." Yum Yum lit a cigarette, its thick and sharp scent a lifeline to Chase's nostrils. He was only fourteen, and while his dad didn't mind him smoking, his grandpa didn't want him to pick up the habit, so he had to refrain from showing too much interest. Boy, he could really use a smoke right now, though. Hadn't had one since sitting on the porch late last night.

Chase caught his grandpa looking out onto the water. The old man's eyes fixed on something.

"What?" Chase asked.

"Bumps on the water. Gators." He looked Chase square in the eye. "Get in the damn boat."

Chase raised a finger. "One sec." He waded around the area, paying careful attention to what was beneath his feet. He only had on a pair of shorts and sneakers with no socks. Feeling things out under the water was easy. He stepped over a sunken log then gave it a tap with his foot to see if it was hollow. Seemed like it. He followed its length in one direction until he came to the end of it.

Yum Yum still gazed out on the water. "Get in the boat, Chase."

"Yeah, yeah." Chase crouched down in the water and felt for the log's opening. Once located, he stuck his hand inside and wriggled his fingers, hoping to catch the attention of something within. While he did, he followed his grandpa's line of sight and saw a couple of alligators swimming along the surface a good distance away. One quickly went under the water. "You got the rifle, right?"

"Ready and loaded," his grandpa said. His cigarette was already burned right down to the filter, but his grandpa was notorious for keeping the thing in his mouth until the cherry quit and he'd just spit it out.

The alligator way over on the other side of the boat resurfaced. It was a little closer, but Chase didn't think he was in danger territory yet.

He kept wriggling his fingers. "Come on, come on." He wanted this catch. *Needed* it. He'd been craving deep-fried catfish since last week. Breaded and greasy deep-fried catfish. Throw some lemon on there and minced garlic—his stomach growled.

"There's three of them now," Yum Yum said. He pulled a paddle from somewhere near his feet and took the boat close to Chase. "Climb in."

Chase didn't respond.

"Hey." Something hard knocked him in the shoulder. It was the paddle. "Next time this goes across your head."

"Two minutes." There had to be a catfish down here. Had to be. He needed that deep fry.

"Two minutes, huh? One for each gator over there. The third went under the water and it was pointed in this direction."

Something latched onto Chase's hand.

He got one.

"Yes!" Chase said. He grabbed the fish good and tight and drew it out of the log.

"Another went under, Chase. Get in the boat!"

Chase pulled on the catfish and brought it out of the water. "See? Ha!"

Yum Yum finally spat out his cigarette then reached over the edge of the boat. "Pass it here."

Chase took hold of the fish so he now had it in both hands. It was probably a thirteen pounder.

His grandpa helped him wrangle its floppy form.

Chase glanced over the water.

The gators were gone.

He didn't know if they were swimming under the water toward them. His heart picked up pace when he suddenly felt exposed. He practically shoved the catfish into his grandpa's hands then placed his palms on the edge of the boat to pull himself in.

The boat rocked, nearly tipping into the water from his weight.

Yum Yum lost his footing. "Hey, take it easy!"

Chase's hands slipped on the edge and he splashed back into the water and went under. When he resurfaced, he saw his grandpa had fallen in the boat, the large catfish on top of him.

Yum Yum tossed the fish off himself then regained his balance and footing. "Ya idiot!" The old man's eyes went back out to the water. Chase followed his gaze. The three gators had resurfaced and were coming toward them.

"Sorry," Chase muttered as he climbed into the boat.

"We're leaving," Yum Yum said.

Chase watched the gators.

They kept swimming their way.

The catfish flipped and flopped hard in the boat.

"Put your fish away," Yum Yum said and made his way over to the onboard motor.

"Does the motor scare the gators?" Chase asked.

"It—" His grandpa cut himself off when he looked in the gators' direction. Chase checked the alligators. They swam along the surface, but had changed direction and were heading away from them. Relief filled him.

His grandpa seemed to have forgotten his reply because he got to work starting the motor. It came to life.

"Does it?" Chase asked.

"Does it what?"

"Not important now 'cause they're already swimming away, but I was wondering if the motor scares them?"

Yum Yum pulled a fresh cigarette from the pack in his pocket. He seemed about to answer when a giant wall of dark green scales sprang from the water and hurdled over the boat, taking Yum Yum with it.

Whatever it was splashed down on the other side and went under; the waves from its impact rocked the boat so bad Chase fell on his ass then another roll of waves sent his feet up in the air and his head smacking against the boat's floor. The catfish bounded on top of him, still flipping around, its bouncing, heavy weight sending dull jolts throughout his ribs. He rolled away from the fish then lay there as the boat rocked with the waves. When it finally settled enough he thought he could stand, he got to his feet.

"Grandpa!" Chase shouted. "Hey!"

The waves around the boat slowly began evening out.

"Yum Yum! Yo, Trev!"

The water was silent. His grandpa was gone.

"What the hell?" he breathed. He checked the water further away. Couldn't see anything. Even the gators were gone.

Panic began to set in.

He looked to the catfish. It was finally settling.

"Grandpa!" Chase screamed out over the water.

He looked in all directions. He hoped he'd see Yum Yum swimming or splashing or standing where it was shallow.

But he didn't.

He was out here alone.

Tears stung his eyes at the thought his grandpa had bit the big one. But from what? What the hell was that thing?

All Chase knew was that it was huge, green, scaly.

A gator?

No way. Not that big. He knew alligators were big in general, but this thing was monstrous. Had to be something else.

Something else that took his grandpa to a watery grave.

Chase sat on the boat's floor and let the tears come. He was raised not to cry, but this was different. His grandpa had been taken from him right in front of his eyes. This wasn't death at a distance.

This just happened.

Right now.

In front of him.

With a . . . thing . . . that he couldn't label or place.

Chase screamed at the sky then looked over the side of the boat. For some reason, he got the mental image of his grandpa surfacing right where his gaze met the water, but all he saw was his murky, rippling reflection.

"Dammit!" he shouted and smacked his fist on the edge of the boat.

The water stirred, and before he could even get a make on what caused it, a giant, scaly mouth with enormous teeth broke the surface and came right for him.

The last sound Chase heard was the crushing of his skull inside the thing's mouth.

1

"Did you bring enough beer?" Jessica asked and pulled her suitcase from the back of Dave's SUV.

"Do gators swim in these waters?" he said.

"Just want to make sure. I don't want to go into town for a beer run half-cut." She giggled and glanced back at him over her shoulder. "Whole cut."

"Aww, but you're so cute when you're drunk."

She gave him a playful smile then waddled with the heavy suitcase to the wooden bridge that connected the shoreline to the house on the water.

Dave was close behind. "What do you got in that thing, a dead body?"

"Girl stuff. Four hair dryers, a vanity, six bottles of hairspray, a manicure set. You know, the usual."

"Ha! You? You're the most non-girl girl I know."

"And you're the most non-guy guy I know."

He came up beside her. "Which is why we work so well together, I suppose." He leaned in and gave her a quick peck.

"Don't start up now. There's not enough time for any fun and games before Chad and Marley get here."

"That's stupid. They're coming this evening."

"Don't you want it all? The appetizer, the main course, pillow talk?"

"I only need ten minutes," he said.

"Well, I need a lot longer than that."

"Yeah, yeah," he muttered.

They headed down the wooden bridge that led to Dave's uncle's water house. Not that "water house" was the technical term, but it was what Dave always called it and the term now stuck with Jessica. His uncle lived here roughly six months out of the year, then went even further south to Mexico for the winter. Not that it got terribly cold here, but Dave's uncle was a sun junkie and had major issues when things cooled down.

Jessica approached the entrance at the side of the cabin and waited for Dave to fish the key out of his pocket. She looked at Dave's backpack. It was all he brought, the beer aside, which was in a giant cooler in the trunk. She'd have to help him lug the cooler to the cabin; the thing was so heavy. She hated the idea of trudging with it to the house, though smirked at the thought of it being empty by the end of the weekend. Dave unlocked the door, and the two went in.

The place was quaint, roughly eight hundred square feet, all one level. It stood on a platform in the water, the platform supported by a series of stilts. As cool as it would've been for this place to be a floating houseboat kind of thing, she was thankful it was more or less anchored. Shuddering images of waking up in the middle of the night only to see they'd drifted somewhere into the middle of the water made her toes curl.

The place was just a square. To her right were the two bedrooms and bathroom. To the left the dining area with the living room just beyond. Straight ahead was the kitchen, which was nothing fancy. From what she understood, a powerline ran down beneath the house then somewhere along the underside of the bridge to a source on land. Didn't seem like a very practical—or even safe— setup, but it worked.

"Here," Dave said and took her suitcase. "I'll toss this on the bed and you can organize your stuff later."

"What if I want to do it now?"

"I thought you said you didn't want to *do it* now?"

"I meant my suitcase, you idiot."

He smiled. "I know. It's called teasing, you know, when someone bugs someone else in jest?"

"Oooh, 'jest.' You don't hear that word that often."

"Thought you'd be impressed."

"Yeah, because it's such a 'big' word."

He frowned.

"That was sarcasm," she said.

He gave an exaggerated sigh then a grin, then took their stuff to the bedroom, leaving her alone.

Jessica went to the fridge to see if Dave's uncle had left anything. It was fairly bare: half a stick of butter, an expired one-litre carton of milk, a bottle of ketchup and a couple odds and ends that would be of little use. Chad and Marley were in charge of the food. Too bad they wouldn't be here until anytime this evening. She hoped Dave had brought something to eat even if just a snack. She had been so busy between work and getting her stuff together to get here that bringing a bite slipped her mind.

Dave came out of the bedroom and stepped up to her and drew her in close.

"Come on, not now," she said.

"What? Can't a guy hug his girl?"

"You want something else."

"I just want you."

"Yeah, I know."

"I meant, I just want *you*. You. You're my special girl." He gave her a dopey grin, but it was that grin that got to her last year. It was that grin that meant he was sincere when he expressed his feelings toward her.

It's not that she was resisting him because she wasn't interested. She was resisting him because they hadn't been intimate in so long and she didn't want to make up for lost time in a place like this. She wanted a hotel with a big soft bed, room service, and an all-you-can buffet downstairs for after they worked up an appetite. Or, maybe, she was just wasn't being considerate of his feelings.

His blue eyes looked into hers.

Those eyes.

Soft, playful, warm. Definitely not the kind of eyes she was used to from the other guys she'd dated over the years.

She leaned against his chest and returned his embrace with a gentle squeeze of her own. After, she looked up and kissed him.

A few moments later, he started to pull away, probably because he didn't want to infringe on any personal space he thought she might want, so she pressed her lips into his, hoping to assure him she cared.

Oh, how she cared.

She might even be in love.

After the kiss, Dave took her hands in his and said, "Want that beer?"

Jessica smiled. "Yes, please."

"Good. They're in the trunk, and I can't carry that cooler on my own." He let go of her hands and headed toward the door.

She rolled her eyes and followed.

* * *

Dave looked at the beer can pyramid he made. He was six in and was pleased he made the three-tiered structure work. It also looked a little blurry, but six beers would do that to you, especially on a near-empty stomach. All he'd brought was a big bag of Doritos, which he and Jessica shared, but that was over the course of five hours, and he'd skipped breakfast today.

Clomping outside told him someone else was on the platform. Hopefully Chad with the grub. Not that he was expecting anybody else.

He stood from the table, swayed a second, then gave his head a quick shake to snap out of it.

Yeah, it'd better be Chad.

"You got it?" Jessica said, looking up from her book while she sat on the old, worn couch in the living room.

"Yep. I got it." He went to the door. "Don't know why they don't just walk in. Told them to come right—" He opened the door.

Giganti-gator Death Machine

It wasn't Chad or Marley.

2

A dude with gray hair and brown eyes stood next to a pretty girl with blonde hair and blue ones.

Dave had no clue who they were. He ran his hand through his hair then scratched the back of his head. "I think you got the wrong house, man."

"You Dave?" the guy asked.

"Yeah."

"Then I got the right one." The guy produced a brown paper bag, which was clearly hiding a bottle. "Here, hold this." He shoved the bag into Dave's hand. "Homemade rum. Top secret recipe. Tell no one."

"Right."

The girl stepped in between the guys. "This is Ian. I'm Alana. We know Chad and Marley. They told us what they were doing this weekend and said we could join them."

Dave didn't know what to say.

"And . . . well, I guess, judging by the look on your face, Chad didn't text you like he said he was going to and tell you we were coming."

"Nope, he didn't," Dave said. "Come on in, I guess." He backed away from the door to give them clearance.

The two entered and set down their things.

Jessica eyed the two strangers from the couch.

Dave thumbed in the newcomer's direction. "This is Ian and Alana. They know Chad. Apparently, they're joining us this weekend."

"Okay, sure," Jessica said, seeming somehow cheerful about it.

It wasn't that having extra people around was a bad thing. Just would've been nice if it'd been people Dave knew.

Ian had already made himself at home in the kitchen and was unpacking several bottles of liquor from a duffle bag. How anyone was gonna drink all that *and* the beer, Dave didn't know.

Upon closer inspection, Dave noticed Ian didn't seem that much older than he was, maybe early thirties. The guy had just gone gray early. Full gray.

Alana was already in the living room chatting with Jessica. Dave stared after them. Jessica could get along with just about anybody and, it seemed, a perfect stranger was no exception.

Ian reached a hand over Dave's shoulder and passed him a glass filled halfway with an amber liquid.

"Spiced rum," Ian said. "Sip it. Don't shoot it. You're welcome."

Dave looked at the contents of the glass. Good or bad, at least the rum would take the edge off having strangers in his uncle's house.

* * *

Chad and Marley finally showed up about an hour later with the food.

Hot dogs never tasted so good, and Jessica hoped no one was looking when she snuck her fourth one. Not long after the late supper settled in her stomach was she ready for another beer. She cracked one open and got to work putting it away. Her buzz had died down and she needed to catch up.

"Who wants to play a board game?" Chad asked.

"A board game? That's so lame," Jessica said.

"Tell that to the multimillionaires who make them."

"Still lame."

"I'd be happy to just to sit and chill," Marley said.

"But you said on the way down here that—" She cut off Chad with an arched eyebrow. "Fine. Whatever," Chad said.

The six of them sat around the table, each with a beer in hand—except for Ian, who had stuck with the hard stuff all night. Jessica figured he was on his fifth whiskey by now. Strangely, the drink didn't make him loud and obnoxious as expected. Ian just kept to himself and only spoke when spoken to.

"So, how do you guys know each other?" Jessica asked and gestured between Chad and Marley and Ian and Alana with her index finger.

"Worked with Ian for a few years when doing that marketing stint downtown," Chad said.

To Ian and Alana, she asked, "You guys been together long or . . ."

Alana looked to Ian. "We've been together for, what, four years? Five?"

"Four," he said. With a smile to everybody else, he added, "Sometimes feels like five."

"Good for you," Jessica said.

"You guys?" Alana asked.

"Dave and I have been together since last year."

Dave simply grinned that dopey grin.

"The beginning of a relationship is always fun," Alana said. "Everything's new and exciting. Nothing's same old, same old yet."

"Never want things to get same old, same old," Jessica said.

"It's inevitable," she replied.

"Not if you change things up. Keep it fresh. And people are multi-faceted so new things are bound to always come up."

Alana thumbed over to Ian. "Not with this guy." She gave him a smile. "Single-faceted in some things, I'd say."

Ian frowned. "Hey." Then smiled.

Jessica took another swig of her beer. It was beginning to lose its flavor, which meant she was well on her way to putting down can after can like water.

Dave knocked off his beer and went to the fridge for another.

"How are we going to work sleeping with only two bedrooms?" Marley asked.

"Two and two in the rooms, then the remaining couple out here," Jessica said.

"And who gets the rooms?"

Jessica thought back to her and Dave already dumping their stuff off in one of the bedrooms. The other four hadn't done that yet, and she'd also feel bad if she said her stuff was already in one, so the others had to flip a coin or something for the last room.

"I'm heading out for a smoke," Dave said, cracking open his beer.

"You don't smoke," Jessica said.

"Here I do. Brought cigars."

"I'll join you," Ian said.

Jessica could tell by Dave's flat expression that he'd been hoping Chad would join him instead of Ian. Dave looked to Chad. Chad gave his head a small shake.

"Anybody else?" Dave asked.

"Nope," Alana said.

"Not me," Marley said.

"No thanks," Jessica said.

"Sigh. Fine," Dave said.

"All right, boyo, just you and me," Ian said, giving Dave's shoulder a slap. "We can solve the secrets of the universe while looking at the stars."

"I guess so."

* * *

Dave watched Ian as the guy took a swig of his beer. Amazing. Just prior to coming outside, Ian must've quickly chugged one down in between doing the hard stuff. Dave could only imagine the carbonated burn.

"So?" Ian asked.

"So, what?" Dave replied.

"I don't know. This is the part where we talk about the weather or something."

"I guess. Um . . . nice night."

Ian looked out over the water. It was calm except for a few ripples. "Sure is. Warm, muggy. Not steam-room weather. Hate that."

"Me, too." Dave took a deep breath then took a sip of his own beer.

Ian had his head tilted back as he finished his beer already, then tossed the can onto the water.

"Hey, don't do that," Dave said.

"Don't think the gators mind."

"Probably not, but that puts crap in the water that's not supposed to be there."

Ian pulled a fresh can out from his pocket. He cracked it open. "They'll live, the world will go on."

"That's not the point."

Ian chuckled loud then gave his can a little shake. "Should shake one of these up real good then throw it in and hope a gator swallows it whole. Wonder if it'll explode on the inside."

Dave smirked. "I don't know, man. Who knows? Still . . ." Ian had obviously let the issue of littering in the water go.

The two stood in silence for a while. The water remained quiet, too, but Dave couldn't help but wonder what lurked beneath its surface. Could be anything; could be nothing. A mental flash of a catfish swimming in the murk went past his mind's eye, then his attention was drawn to a sudden splash on the water somewhere over on the right.

"Someone's gone swimming," Ian said.

"Someone?"

"Or a big ol' garfish did a hop out of the water and kaplooshed back in."

"Those are those ones with alligator faces, right?"

"Something like that. I don't know. Maybe."

Not a big help, Dave thought. "I should probably get back in to Jess."

"On a leash?"

Dave frowned. "No. Just we came out here to spend time together, so I should probably be doing that."

"Do you want to?"

"Of course I want to. What kind of question is that?"

Ian put his hands up in false surrender. "Hey, man, look, was just saying stuff."

"Yeah, saying stuff," Dave muttered.

"Go back in. I'm gonna stay out here awhile."

Dave nodded. "Sure. Have a good one." He turned to go back in then glanced over his shoulder at the water. Could've been the subtle waves, but he thought he saw a couple dark bumps moving along its surface.

3

Later, Jessica stood at the railing overlooking the water and took in the starlight above. The humid night breeze ran over her skin like warm fingertips. She wore a purple bikini beneath a baggy white T-shirt.

She waved Dave over. "Come on," she whispered.

Dave stepped up behind her. "This is crazy."

"What? You've never been skinny dipping before?"

"Does the bathtub count?"

She gave him a playful shove. "Not a chance." She leaned a bit over the railing. The water was pitch black.

"I really don't think this is a good idea," Dave said. "There're things in that water that aren't too friendly."

"Come on. It'll be just a quick in-and-out." She reached down and grabbed the T-shirt by the hem then pulled it up and over her body. Judging by the way Dave's jaw slightly dropped, she knew he liked what he saw. "You, too, Mister, come on," she said, pointing to his T-shirt.

"Sigh. Fine." Dave took his shirt off.

Jessica turned away from him and undid her bikini top. It's not like Dave hadn't seen her topless before, but she liked teasing him. Still hiding her breasts, she glanced over her shoulder. "Your turn."

Dave rolled his eyes. "All right, all right." He dropped his bathing suit in a heap around his ankles. Guys never had any grace when it came to seduction.

Still, she smiled. She removed her own bottoms, gave her backside a little sway, then went to the opening between the railing where a ladder led into the water.

She dove in. The water was fresh and cool. She thought if only those sleeping inside of the cabin knew what was going on . . .

Dave got to the opening between the railing and climbed down the ladder. Extra boring. She had hoped he'd dive in or jump or do something more exciting than that.

She swam up to him and pressed her body against his and gave him a peck on the lips. "See? Fun."

He did that dopey smile of his then kissed her back.

The two swam out further from the cabin, taking turns going under the water and seeing who could swim the farthest beneath the surface without taking a breath. Dave won a couple times; she won four. Though the stars and moon above provided some light, the cabin was starting to get lost in the distant shadows. Dave was fairly far away, too, but closer to the cabin.

"Jess!" he shouted. His voice barely carried on the air.

She swam closer so she could hear him better. "Yeah?"

"Jess, behind you!"

She turned around to see some sort of dark lump moving across the top of the water. At first, she thought it was a giant log just floating along the surface, but the thing had a trajectory and was headed straight for her.

"Jess! Swim!" Dave shouted. At first glance, it looked like Dave was going to swim away from her, but then changed direction and started coming out to her. He kicked and splashed so hard in the water that all she read off him was panic. "Hurry! Swim!"

Jess kicked it into high gear and started heading toward Dave all the while checking over her shoulder now and then. That log thing grew in size and lost any possibility of randomness to its float.

It wasn't a log.

It was alive.

Gator! One hell of a gator! she thought.

Suddenly shrieking, she scrambled through the water, trying her best to get to Dave as soon as possible.

She glanced over her shoulder again and saw the gator slip beneath the surface. *Oh no.* Now it could be anywhere.

"Jess!" Dave finally caught up to her and grabbed her.

She sobbed and cried into his shoulder. "Where is it? Where is it? Where is it?" Panic taking over, her heart in overdrive, she clawed and pulled at him and accidentally dunked him under the water. When he resurfaced, he grabbed her hard by the shoulders and gave her a shake.

"Stop it!" he shouted. He took her by the arm and led her toward the safety of the cabin.

The bumpy lump resurfaced over to her left not more than twenty or so feet away.

Screaming, she climbed onto Dave and pushed him under the water again. This time, when he came back up, he gave her a hard swat across the shoulder, sending a shock of pain down her arm. At first, she was pissed at him hitting her, then realized he was trying to jolt her back to reality.

"Swim. Swim. Swim," he told her.

They swam as fast as they could toward the railing.

The gator pursued . . . and picked up speed.

They were almost at the ladder.

"Move it, Jess! Move it!" Dave said.

Tears blurring her vision, her limbs wobbly from the adrenaline, she started to flounder and momentarily went under the water. From beneath the surface she heard Dave's muffled voice call her name. When she popped back up above the water, the gator's body surfaced in all fullness. It was difficult to tell in the dark, but the thing looked to be at least sixty or more feet long and possibly seven or eight feet wide. Its mouth came at her open full and wide and plowed right into her. Its fangs raked across her skin and it scooped her inside. Somewhere behind her Dave screamed for help and called her name.

The gator's teeth mashed down on her, giant spikes that cut straight through her arms, at first breaking through the bones then severing them completely. She felt the blood run from her extremities and the awful sucking feeling on her legs as her body was drawn down the thing's throat.

4

"Jess! Jess!" Dave screeched. He peered over the railing into the water. Nothing but murky water stared back. "Jess, where are you! Jess!" He ran to the far side of the railing and looked out that way. "Jess!" He stared out onto the water. There was a dark patch floating along its surface.

Blood.

"Jess!"

He hardly heard the scrambled thumping of footsteps on wood before Chad came up beside him. "Dude, what's going on?"

Dave's voice was laced with tears. "Jess . . . oh, Jess." He gathered his breath. "Jess!"

"Easy, man, easy," Chad said.

Soon Marley, Ian, and Alana were all on the deck beside him.

"It was . . . it was . . ." Dave could barely speak. He screamed at the night sky. "Jess!"

"You're shaking," Ian said and put a hand on Dave's shoulder. His mere touch made Dave recoil. "And you're naked."

One of the girls giggled. Dave didn't know which one.

"Let's get you inside," Ian said.

"No," Dave said. "Not without Jess. Not without my Jessica."

"Come on," Ian said and fully put his arm around Dave's shoulder.

Dave shrugged it off. "Touch me again and I'll kill you."

"Hey!" Chad said. "Take it easy."

"Shut up," Dave snapped. "We were . . . we were just . . . just swimming and then this . . . oh no . . . this gator came and just . . ." The tears fell. When he composed himself, he said, "It ate her."

"Gator?" Marley said. "As in alli*gator*?"

Dave merely nodded. He suddenly felt his nakedness and put his hands over his privates.

"Come on," Chad said gently, "let's go inside. No sense being out here."

This time Dave let himself be guided toward the cabin door but still kept an eye over his shoulder. That thing was out there.

That thing that ate Jessica.

* * *

All of them sat around the table. Dave was dressed now in a pair of sweatpants and a T-shirt. Everyone else had some version of pajamas on. Dave's clothes didn't stop him from shaking, though.

"Are you sure you saw what you thought you saw?" Alana asked.

Dave simply nodded.

"How big was it?"

Dave slowly shook his head. "I don't know. Massive. Too massive. People-eating-size massive." He couldn't believe he said that last part. More tears leaked from his eyes.

Everyone went quiet, and Dave didn't know if it was because of sympathy for him or to mourn Jessica or fear this giant alligator was out there, or some kind of weird combination of all three.

"We can't stay here," Marley said matter-of-factly as she stared at the table. "We have to get out."

"Gators stay in the water, Marley," Ian said.

"Not if they're on land, which they can do, by the way," she shot back.

"He's not going to get in here."

"So, what, we just stay inside the cabin and pretend nothing happened to Jessica and play board games and get drunk all weekend?"

"That's not what I meant."

"Guys," Dave said, "I just lost my girlfriend. Show some respect."

There was silence for a few moments before Chad asked, "So what do you want to do, Dave?"

He thought about it for a moment. A part of him wanted to run for the hills; another part wanted to curl into a ball under the covers and pretend Jessica's death didn't happen. His soul might've been crushed, but he knew what they should do. "We need to pack up and leave and tell the sheriff or animal control or some kind of authority person what happened." He put his head in his hands. "I don't know." He looked up. "What do you do in a situation like this?"

No one had an answer.

It was then the entire cabin shook as if the whole thing got hit with a giant battering ram. Nearly all of them fell off their seats.

"What the hell?" Ian said.

They all got to their feet.

The cabin lurched again and a quick mental flash of a freight train slamming the stilts that held the place above water went through Dave's brain.

Another hit, and they all went tumbling to the floor. The distinct-yet-muted sound of wood snapping confirmed Dave's mental image: that giant gator was taking out the poles that kept the cabin stationary on the water. He didn't know exactly how many there were, but those anchored the place to the lakebed. The other anchoring point was the wooden bridge that ran off the deck that surrounded the place and hooked onto the mainland.

Another slam, this one far away from them on the side of the cabin that overlooked the lake.

Dave caught Alana's wide-eyed gaze.

Another hit, this one more slow and methodical. Dave heard the dull crunching of wood beneath the cabin's floor and suspected the gator was chewing its way through the posts. How many of the posts the thing had taken out so far was anybody's guess.

All went still and everyone remained motionless, bracing for another impact.

None came.

Marely's choppy breathing from the onslaught set Dave on edge. Chad must've sensed it, too, because he said, "Deep breaths, Marl. Deep breaths. Slowly. Calmly."

Another big hit and everyone was on all fours as the cabin fell off its supports and splashed into the water. They all gripped the floor however they could as the cabin rocked side to side and front to back.

Then all went motionless again.

Dave's eyes went to each of them. Marley had tears and was gripped with fear. Alana the same. Chad had this expression that read he thought he knew what he should do but didn't. Ian had his brow furrowed, the seemingly calmest of the bunch.

Please no more, please no more, Dave thought.

The cabin gently rocked on the waves.

Ian said, "Careful, single file, to the door. I'll go first and take a look outside. If that bridge is still intact or somehow hanging on, we make a break for it and get onto solid land. Leave our stuff. Let's just get the hell out of here."

Dave nodded his concurrence, then thought back to Jessica and the blood on the water.

5

Ian slowly opened the door and checked outside. All was quiet. Not even a ripple on the water so far as he could tell. Good sign. He glanced back over his shoulder. Everyone else was crouched down in a row behind him, presumably staying low to the floor in case the cabin started rocking again.

He made a silent hand gesture pointing left then right then gave a thumbs up. Alana nodded her understanding. The others didn't acknowledge. He gave the thumbs up again, and this time Dave nodded.

To the left was the decking that rounded back to the rear of the cabin and the bridge. He wasn't sure if they should all go out at once or just him to make sure the coast was clear. He decided it best they all go together: leave no man behind.

He waved them on.

Slowly, everyone made their way on hands and knees or duck-walked along the decking. He checked back on them again. Dave and Marley kept glancing left and right with Dave keeping a particular eye on the water's surface. The bridge wasn't that far away but was around the far corner of the cabin. It would only be there he could take a closer look and see if the thing was still attached. He braced himself for the gator's impact at any moment, but the further they moved along, none came. Finally, they reached the end of the decking. He peered around the corner. There was the bridge and, despite the shadows, it still seemed locked onto the main deck surrounding the cabin.

Whispering, he said, "We have to do this quickly. On the count of three, get up and just give 'er and run as far inland as you can. We'll regroup there." He looked at each face to make sure they all understood. Some nodded. Dave said, "Yep."

Dave looked at the water again, and Ian's heart went out to him. Poor Jessica.

Alana was right behind Ian. "Love you, babe," he said.

"Love you, too," she replied.

He gave her hand a thoughtful squeeze, then raised his gaze to the others. "On three." He slowly inhaled then exhaled. "One, two . . . three." He got his feet under him as fast as he could and charged for the bridge. Behind him, he heard clunking, and while he made a break for it, he saw Alana had stumbled and everyone else had crashed into her.

"Get up! Get up! Get up!" he shouted and planted his foot on the bridge. He gave it all he had. The water brewed beside him, and his heart leapt in his chest. Like a mountain of reptile skin and muscle, the gator dove out of the water, mouth open, and clamped around Ian's middle. As they crashed into the water, he saw the bridge was cut in two, wooden boards and large splinters going up like fireworks.

The gator thrashed him about in the water, biting down ever harder against his body. Its vice-like grip kept squeezing as those massive teeth shredded him through his belly. He even felt—and heard—the teeth bang together as he was torn clean in two. His breathing stopped, the bottoms of his lungs no doubt torn open like wet paper bags. Just over to his left his legs floated away atop the water.

The others screamed from the deck.

"Ian!" Alana cried.

His arms went numb, and the gator's mouth opened wide and came at him full force, swallowing his upper body whole.

* * *

"No!" Alana screamed so hard her voice scraped the inside of her throat. She reached out to where the bridge was broken off the deck as if she could somehow reach Ian himself inside the gator's body.

Where was it? Where did it go? The gator was back under the water, leaving nothing but a trashed bridge and Ian's legs floating on the water's surface. Those legs . . .

The gator burst from beneath the water's surface and swallowed those, too, in one giant gulp.

"No!" she screamed, crying—bawling—"Ian!" Someone grabbed her from behind. It was Dave. She shook in his arms.

"Get back, get back, get back," he said.

The gator resurfaced again, this time revealing its massive body as it did a kind of figure eight atop the water as if showing off its power.

It was hard to see it in its entirety under the moonlight, but the thing was absolutely gigantic. It was like three adult gators strung together, and for a brief second, Alana thought that's what it was. Was it? Had it been three all along? But there weren't three heads. There weren't three tails. Just one long giant beast made of dark, thick reptilian hide.

"I want to go inside," Marley said. "I want to go inside."

Good idea, Alana thought. She looked at them and wondered why they hadn't heard her, then realized she had thought the words instead of said them. "Go," she said between panted breaths. "Go. In. Side."

Dave pulled at her while Marley and Chad headed back toward the cabin door. Alana wasn't sure being inside the cabin was any safer, but it beat being out here out in the open exposed to the alligator.

This time, they didn't crawl or duck walk but instead ran with all their might. Alana's legs were like Jell-O, and she had to lean on Dave to keep from collapsing. When they all made it back inside, Chad leaned up against the door and locked it. He then patted up and down where the door met the frame, and Alana could only presume he was checking for other locks—which clearly weren't there, but it showed where his panic level was.

They all quickly stumbled into the living room and fell to the floor, every one of them either laying down or curled up in a ball, trembling from the adrenaline. Nothing but panicked, panting breaths filled the air.

Alana cried. So did Marley, and though she couldn't be sure, she thought she heard the guys crying as well.

Ian . . . her sweet Ian—dead.

They all lay there for who knew how long until the entire cabin shook again as if the gator was making one final statement it was in charge and there was nothing they could do about it.

6

Chad awoke to the sound of Alana sniffling. The others were still laying on the floor, sleeping. The morning light came through the cabin's windows. Before he moved, he stared down at the floor and imagined the murky water beneath and the possibility the gator was right beneath them, swimming in circles, just biding its time before it would strike. From what he recalled from a fitful night's rest, no other impacts came, but the adrenaline drain had been so strong he could've slept through anything.

That's not true, he thought. An impact from the gator would've surely woken him and the others.

Alana still sniffled.

He moved over to her and put a hand on her shoulder. She recoiled a little from his touch. Still jumpy.

"Hey, it's okay," he said as soothingly as he could.

"No, it's not okay," she said, her tone like venom. "Ian's dead. Jessica's dead. We're all gonna be dead."

He breathed in slow then sighed. "You don't know that."

"There were six of us. Two of us are gone. What do you think's gonna happen? We're trapped in here like some stupid chicken coop. That thing out there . . . it'll kill us all, you know?"

"You don't know that," he said again.

"The bridge is gone. Whatever the hell wood things that held this place up are all broken. We're probably floating in the middle of the lake." She looked up at him with tear-stained eyes. "Are we, Chad? Are we floating in the middle of the lake?"

He shook his head. "I don't know."

"Can you check?"

His heart sank at the prospect, but he'd do it for her. He got up and went to the window and peered out. Yes, they were on the water—but the cabin had always been on the water.

"So?" she said.

"Let me check the other side." He crossed the cabin and went into one of the bedrooms, which were the rooms closest to land. He looked out the window. The decimation to the bridge was even more clear in the daylight. Only a small portion of it still clung to the mainland. There was barely any of it left attached to the decking that rimmed the cabin. There was a huge gap between the two. He couldn't recall the exact measurements of the bridge while it was all one piece, so couldn't one hundred percent say if they had floated out any further. He thought it best to just play it calm and assure Alana they were still where they'd always been.

He came out of the bedroom and said, "We're okay. I don't think we've moved."

"How will we get out of here? We can't swim. Not with that thing out there."

"I'm not sure," he said. "Let's just slow down and wake up and wait for the other two to get up as well." He crawled down on the floor beside her and laid his head on his arms.

"You're not going to go back to sleep, are you?"

He closed his eyes. "No. Just resting. Just thinking. Try and do the same. We need to stay calm otherwise we'll drag all of us down."

She nodded her agreement.

Dave let out a snore.

That made Alana giggle for some reason.

Chad smiled.

It was good to see a ray of sunshine in all this.

* * *

Marley peeked her head around the door and looked at the decimated bridge and portions of the torn-up decking. Heart sinking, she looked the other way to see Chad looking out over the water.

"Psst, hey, what are you doing?" she whispered as loudly as she could.

He didn't seem to have heard her.

"Hey, Chad," she whispered louder.

He turned back to look at her and waved her over.

"Are you kidding?" she said, still whispering. "I ain't going out there."

"It's fine," he said quietly. "Nothing out here."

She glanced back inside the cabin where Alana and Dave were still sleeping. Cautiously, she stepped out onto the deck and went over to him. He put his arm around her.

"What are you doing out here?" she asked.

"Just looking, thinking if that thing is still out there." He smiled at her. "Maybe it swam away."

As if, she thought. "Or maybe it's swimming close by."

"You can't think like that. Need to stay positive."

"Positive? Are you crazy? That thing just ate two of our friends . . . group . . . whatever." She stayed quiet for a moment, then asked, "What are you really doing out here?"

He sighed. "As morbid as it sounds, I was looking to see if there was still blood on the water. Jessica's blood. Thought maybe if there was, that thing would definitely be circling around."

She took a look for herself but didn't see anything. "Is there?"

"Naw. All washed away, which I suppose is a good thing."

She nodded. "Wish I could see through the water, beneath the surface."

"Don't we all. If this were a clear lake, that would make this a whole lot easier."

"Not really. It'd still be swimming around us, ready to strike at any moment."

"At least we'd be prepared for it."

He was right about that, but how could you prepare to take on an alligator never mind one that was at least triple the size of a regular one? Maybe even quadruple. How'd that thing get so big, anyway?

She studied Chad's face as he studied the water. His jaw was set firm, eyes slightly squinted. What was he thinking? A part of her wanted to know, and a part of her didn't.

"We can't stay here," he finally said.

"Nope. We can't."

"Unless we make some sort of raft, the only way back to the mainland is to swim it."

She shook her head. "I ain't going in there. You kidding?"

"What if we swim real fast, just really give 'er?"

"Give her what? A fresh meal?"

He narrowed his eyes at her. "You know that's not what I meant."

"I know, but it also kind of was. Put any one of us in the lake—whether one at a time or all at once—and someone's going down. I mean" —she thought for a moment— "if we all went in, it wouldn't attack us all at once. I don't think, I mean."

"Marley." He said her name firmly.

"Sorry. Dumb idea."

"I think a raft is our best bet. Let's go inside and see what we have. Might be some tools in there."

"Might be."

"A raft could be our only hope."

7

Later, Chad and Dave rummaged around the place, looking for anything they could use to build a raft. Even if it wasn't that big and could only carry one or two of them at a time, it didn't matter. As long as eventually the four of them made it to the mainland.

"We could flip the table over and use that. Ready-built," Dave said.

"Think it'd have enough buoyancy?" Chad asked.

Dave pounded his fist on the tabletop. "Seems solid enough. Thick enough, too. That's three or four inches of solid wood. The table legs would be something to hold on to. Tie a rope—if we have one—and have the first guy paddle it across. Those left can haul the table back with the rope, rinse and repeat."

"No water jokes, please," Chad said.

"I didn't mean—"

Chad just waved him off with a flip of the hand. "Sorry. Just tired and concerned."

"At least you didn't lose your girl to a giant gator."

"Again, sorry."

The two guys stayed quiet. The bro code. Most tense moments were solved with a moment of silence.

"I'll check again for some tools," Dave said, "but I didn't see anything on my first pass. Maybe Uncle Rick didn't keep much on hand. I don't know."

He went around the cabin, looking in every drawer and every closet. Even under the beds, and came up empty. The only thing of use he did find was a .22 rifle and a three-quarter-full box of bullets. He presented it to Chad. "We got this."

"Think you could align a headshot if it came to it?" Chad said.

"I've rarely shot these things. Have an aversion to guns."

Chad gave him a look like he was crazy.

"What? You a gun nut?" Dave asked.

Chad took the rifle in his hands and looked down the barrel. "I've shot my fair share."

"Then I'll leave you in charge of that unless it so happens I need it or even the girls."

Alana came up to them. "A .22. Nice." She took it from Chad and repeated his gaze down the barrel. "Ka-boom."

Dave shoved the barrel away from his vicinity. "Don't point this thing at people."

"Why? It's not loaded. See?" She popped the safety off and pulled the trigger. A blast rang out as a bullet pierced the floor. Marely yelped from the other room. "Oops. Sorry."

Chad yanked the gun away from her. "Not cool. First we got alligators eating people and now we could've been shooting each other. You're not touching this."

"Sheesh, I said I was sorry," she said and huffed off.

"I hate guns," Dave said.

Chad merely raised his eyebrows.

* * *

In lieu of a rope, they strung together as many bed-sheets as they could find, twisting them first then tying them as tightly together as possible. Getting the kitchen table out the door was a bit of a trick because the legs were bolted on good and tight and they had nothing they could loosen them with to help make the job easier. After several tries, Chad and Dave were finally able to angle the thing around the doorframe and get it out onto the deck. They brought it where the bridge had been ripped apart from the decking and flipped it over. It sat unevenly across the torn-up deck boards. They tied one end of the bedsheet rope around one of the legs good and tight several times to ensure it was locked on and not going anywhere. They were also able to locate an old hockey stick, which was the closest thing they could find to a paddle.

Now it was just a question of who was going first.

"Ladies first," Alana said.

"It's also a risk," Dave said. "As much as I'm all for chivalry, you go out there and if that thing is there, then there's not much we can do for you other than try and pull you in as fast as possible."

She crossed her arms and frowned at that reality.

Conversely, Dave thought, if one of the men went out first and made it, then that was kind of the opposite of being a knight in shining armor. Further, should they take the rifle with them as they went across? If someone got across safely, they could shoot at the creature from the mainland. If something happened, the rifle would be ruined if it hit the water even if they recovered it.

"Someone should have the rifle aiming from here," Dave said. "Chad, that should be your job given that you said you have experience with guns."

"I'll grab it and get it ready," he replied and headed back to the cabin.

Marley had her hands on her hips. "So, who's going first?"

"Still deciding," Dave said.

"And who made you the decision-maker?"

"This is not the time to fight. I just want to make sure we do this as safely as possible." He looked onto the water for the umpteenth time again, checking for any scaly lumps floating along the murky surface. So far, the coast was clear. He looked down at the tabletop raft just as Chad came out with the rifle. "I guess the only thing left to do is give it the ol' heave-ho."

Chad went to move to help, but didn't seem to know what to do with the rifle in the meantime, so Alana took the initiative and helped Dave get the upside-down table onto the water. It hit with a splash.

"We still haven't decided who's going first," Alana said.

"I'll go," Dave said. "That way, if something happens, then it's me and you guys are still safe."

"Not on your life," Marley said.

Poor choice of words, Dave thought.

She shoved past him and jumped onto the table.

"Get back here," Chad said.

"Not happening. Hand me the hockey stick."

Alana picked it up off the deck. "Fine. Your funeral."

"Alana," Dave snapped.

"What? If she wants to die, she can go right ahead."

Where was this coming from? Probably over the death of Ian.

"Just give me the damn stick," Marley said, her hand extended out to receive it. There was no use fighting her.

It was decided, then.

She would go first.

8

Marley tried to balance herself on the upside-down table top. It sort of worked, though some smelly lake water spilled up and over the bracing on the sides. She hoped too much didn't come onto the wood otherwise it might be enough to sink the thing.

"You okay?" Chad shouted from the decking.

Marley spread out on all fours to keep the thing steady. "Yeah, I'll manage." She had yet to figure out how she could maintain her balance and use the hockey stick as a paddle. Once it felt like the table was sturdy enough beneath her, she reached for the hockey stick with her right hand then slowly sat up and got her knees under her.

Okay, nice and slow, she thought.

"I'm gonna start feeding you the line," Dave said, already letting some slack from the bedsheet rope into the water.

"Fine," was all Marley said.

Carefully, she dipped the hockey stick into the water and was mindful to keep the blade angled in such a way it actually did its job of pushing the water behind her. She stroked the water a few times on one side then repeated it on the other.

"You okay there, Marley?" Alana called out.

She didn't reply but simply nodded, her concentration too focused on the task at hand. She hoped Alana saw her confirmation that all was well.

So far.

For a brief moment, she forgot about the alligator lurking somewhere beneath the water's surface. Then reality kicked in, and she kept an eye out in as many directions as she could. She didn't see anything, not even little reptilian bumps from small gators poking their head above the surface.

The faint sound of a trawling motor rose up on the air and got louder somewhere over to her left. She took a glance. Coming around the bend were a couple of young guys in a small fishing boat. At first, it looked like they were going to just troll on by, but when one looked her way then nudged the other, they changed course and moved in their direction. Marely noticed Alana, Chad, and Dave all look in the newcomers' direction. Chad lowered the rifle, assumingly hoping not to alarm them.

The guys pulled up pretty close, maybe around twenty-five feet away.

Her first thought was they could give them all a ride across.

"Hey, watchya do—" one guy started to say.

Chad cut him off. "Get us across and we'll explain later."

"I ain't getting' nobody across until one of yous tell me why she's on a—what's that?—table? And trying to get across."

Marley suddenly burst into tears and she didn't know why. "Please, just help. Get us across. There's a giant alligator in the water."

The guy snorted a laugh. So did his friend. "Um . . . yeah. There's gators all over here." It seemed it was only now he caught sight of the decimated bridge and Marley could see the tumblers turning inside the guy's head. "You ain't having had trouble with one, have you?"

Dave shouted. "Trouble. Massive trouble. Just get us across. There's this huge gator that came along and ate our friends."

The other guy in the boat finally spoke up. "All in one bite, too, I'm sure."

"Not kidding, dude. Get us across."

The guy in the boat dug around for something out of eyeshot near his feet. It was a can, probably a beer. He chugged it then tossed the can into the water. He then reached for the motor and trawled the boat closer.

Alana shouted over the sound of the motor: "Please, help."

The guy in charge of the motor looked to his friend.

Marley's makeshift raft rose up beneath her and she grabbed on with both hands to stabilize the thing. All she could think was: *Uh oh*.

A giant wave gathered up and around the dudes in the boat.

Chad had his rifle up. "Look out!"

The guy who'd just finished his beer looked at the giant wave. Even from Marley's perspective, she saw a set of giant jaws protrude from the wall of water and go slamming through the guy as the giant alligator plowed up and over the boat. It took the last three-quarters of the boat with it, smashing it to smithereens.

Chad fired off a shot into the wall of water but obviously didn't hit anything. Even if he did, it didn't seem to make a dent because the moment the gator splashed on the other side of the boat, it did a quick swirl around in the water and dove up and devoured the other guy in one bite. As its teeth came down around the body, blood and tissue sprayed outward in a gooey mist like silly string and dry ice at the same time.

Marley and Alana both shrieked. Marley could barely see through her tears.

"Shoot the damn thing," she heard Dave yell.

Another shot went off, but Marley couldn't tell in which direction or even if it hit anything.

"Come on! Shoot!" Dave shouted.

"Fire the gun!" Alana screamed so loud her voice was hoarse.

Chad didn't say a word and kept firing in the general direction where the gator had taken the two guys down but was no longer seen above the water's surface.

Marley reached for the hockey stick paddle and stuck it in the water and began paddling like mad. She did it with such abandon she no longer properly scooped the water with the stick's blade and instead just dug it into the murky depth and got nowhere fast. Heart pounding, tears still leaking from her eyes, she chucked the hockey stick aside into the water then, as fast as she could, reached to one side of the table then the other, using her own hands as paddles. She gained a few inches moving forward, but not nearly enough or even fast enough to bring her any hope.

"Dammit! Dammit! Dammit!" she said with each stroke.

The others shouted behind her—yells and screams—but her thoughts were so scrambled she couldn't decipher what they were saying.

"—ator!" came one voice.

Marley looked over her shoulder and the gator's enormous head was up and out of the water. It came crashing down onto the table, bouncing her up and into the air like a see-saw. Her arms and legs flailed as she rode the air then came splashing into the lake. Treading water, heart pounding, limbs already going numb from all the adrenaline, she got an eye on the shoreline and started frantically dog paddling for it.

"Marley! Marley!" Alana screamed.

"No!" It was Chad. More gunfire but it was all just sound behind her.

"Swim! Go!" It was Dave.

Alana shriek-cried. Marley couldn't tell if Alana was calling out her name or some sort of instruction. She didn't care. She just had to make it to shore.

"Go! Go! Go!" she shouted at herself.

The gator surfaced and came in like a rocket from the side. Its huge teeth tore through Marley's legs like they were wet paper towels, leaving nothing but shredded red ribbons that floated to the surface. Marley thought she felt her heart stop at the sight. Warmth escaped somewhere beneath her, and she knew it was her blood. There was also the coolness of the water tickling her exposed flesh.

Blood.

So much blood.

The water was brick red all around her.

Her arms went heavy, and she was certain this time that her heart did indeed stop.

Her friends still shouted something from the decking but their voices began to fade to somewhere in the background.

Her eyes drooping as she bobbed in the water, she lazily looked over to her left and saw a couple of blood-stained teeth coming right for her face.

9

Chad fell back onto the decking. He didn't say anything. Tears filled his eyes, and all he could think about was Marley and the beast that rose out of the water and devoured her. The image played over and over in his mind. Sometimes it played out just like it happened: her on the table, the gator coming right for her and cutting her in half. Other times he saw himself shooting from the safety of the deck and taking the thing out with a bullet or two to its head. Yet other times he saw himself diving into the water and swimming out to her at warp speed and pulling her back to the safety of the deck and cabin. But mostly it was the image of the gator cutting right through her and removing those beautiful legs from her body, the blood pooling and rising to the water's surface, shreds of her thighs and calves floating on the water like strings. Then the gator coming around again and biting her gorgeous face from what was left of her body and eating her completely.

He heard voices, there, somewhere in the background. Screaming ones. One low, one high.

Eventually, they came into focus.

"Get up, get up, get up." It was Dave. Yeah, that was his name. Dave.

Some incoherent shrieking. Female. What was her name, again? Alayna?

Alana.

Strong hands dug hard under his armpits as Dave hoisted him and dragged him back to his feet.

Chad shook the tears from his eyes first then wiped the remainder away with his forearm. Not far from them the big alligator swam in circles, its enormous body just a giant swirl of scales and muscle like some gigantic Ouroboros that had nothing but death on its mind.

Somewhere in the chaos of his thoughts he thought of the rifle and went to reach for it, but couldn't locate it. Alana had it and she sent shot after shot into the thing. Some bullets hit, others sent up spiky splashes of water. Hitting and shooting wild probably wouldn't get her anywhere, but he didn't have the strength to speak. Not after Marley . . . his sweet Marley . . . getting eaten by the creature.

Finally, Dave yanked the gun away from her.

"What are you doing? You crazy? You're wasting all the ammo," he said.

"Give me the damn gun!" she shouted and took hold of it.

Dave yanked on it hard, and after a quick tug-of-war, pulled it away from her.

Chad's legs wobbled beneath him, and he slowly stepped backward further and further away from the beast on the water.

Dave took aim, and Chad had enough of a moment of clarity to see Dave was taking careful time to line up his shot.

Dave fired.

It seemed the bullet hit the creature directly in the head—but to no avail. Its hide was too thick.

Bulletproof.

Chad wanted to take the gun for himself, take aim for himself, and riddle the gator with holy terror and pay it back for stealing his Marley from him. But he couldn't. He just . . . couldn't. His arms hung limp at his sides and his heart bathed in shame for being so weak at a moment he should have been so strong.

He was supposed to have been Marley's hero.

Instead, he was Marley's coward.

Dammit.

The gator stopped its swirling in the water and made a direct line for them, its giant mouth open showing off its giant teeth. All three of them jumped back when the gator crashed into the decking and bit down on the wood. It crunched down so hard on the wood it was like a rabid dog taking on more bone than it could possibly chew.

The gator didn't care.

It backed up and came at them again, smashing its teeth and face into the decking.

The floating cabin rocked and tipped, and water splashed up onto the deck boards.

"Keep backing up," Dave said as another slam from the gator sent the whole thing reeling. "We're giving it bait. Get back and inside as fast as possible. Maybe out of sight, out of mind will work on this thing."

"It's like it's calcu—" Alana was cut short when the gator plowed into the deck again, this time taking a huge chunk of it away, nearly right up to the cabin wall itself.

The three stepped back as fast as they could, balancing each other when one moved too quickly for the others.

"Get in the damn door," Chad said and had a quick moment of pride his voice was finally working.

He shoved Alana through the entrance. Dave fired off another round from the rifle for some reason, though his target wasn't apparent and it seemed more out of panic than actual purpose.

Chad fell into the cabin between the doorframe and Dave stumbled in soon after. Dave went for the door and slammed it closed and leaned up tight against it as Chad fumbled for the locks.

"Block it with something," Dave said, still leaning up against the door.

Chad looked around. So did Alana.

"Grab the couch," Chad said.

"I'm not strong enough to lift that thing," she replied.

"Just grab the damn couch!"

The cabin rocked as the gator slammed into it. Chad looked toward the front where the bedrooms were and for a moment wouldn't have been surprised had the beast come crashing through the walls and began chomping its way through the floorboards to finally get to them.

It might even do that, he thought.

Dave and Alana were suddenly missing, and he caught sight of them grabbing the couch—one on either end—and awkwardly shuffling its weight over to the door. When they finally got there, Chad moved to give them enough room to set the thing in front good and tight. It wasn't an impenetrable barricade, but it might be enough to at least keep the door from accidentally swinging open.

The cabin rocked again, this time sending all three to the ground. Chad landed on all fours. Dave did a face plant and the second he raised his head blood leaked from his nose. Alana simply landed on her ass but must have hit her tailbone because the face she made followed by a yelp showed nothing but sheer pain.

"Stay low," Dave said. "It can't see us anymore."

"What are you, some alligator expert now?" Alana said.

This wasn't the time for snark. "Quiet!" Chad snapped. She shot him a scowl.

All remained still for a few minutes until from somewhere underneath them around the middle of the cabin was a huge bump, as if the thing was trying to come up directly beneath them.

"Crapcrapcrap!" Alana said.

It looked like Dave was about to say something but instead pressed his lips together.

The three stayed as low as possible. Chad's heart thundered in his chest and once again images of Marley being torn in two filled his mind's eye. He then imagined the damn gator directly beneath him and bursting through the floor and dragging him down to watery hell and ripping him to pieces.

Another bump in the middle of the floor, this one lighter than the first.

"Goawaygoawaygoaway," Alana said softly, her lips pressed to the floor.

Chad found himself joining her. "Goawaygoawaygoaway."

Dave remained quiet.

Go away.

Go away.

Go away.

10

The gator never returned. A full day had passed and Dave, Chad, and Alana spent most of their time eating the supplies they brought and playing truth or dare. Dave thought the game inappropriate given the circumstances, yet he thought it completely appropriate *because* of the circumstances. Some humor in all this helped take his mind off Jessica and the creature lurking around out there.

"Wonder if it can smell the food?" Alana had asked at one point.

"Don't know," Chad had said.

"Probably," Dave had said. Gators were known for their sense of smell and given the size of the thing and how many olfactory nerves it must have, not only did it probably smell the food through the flooring of the cabin, but it probably smelled *them* as well.

"Rather not think about it," Chad said.

"Me neither," Alana said.

A few times they thought they felt the cabin bump, but instead realized it was the hard sloshing of the waves against the cabin's decking and sides causing the issue.

Later, when Dave looked out the window, he saw how far they floated out from the mainland. It was still a swimmable distance—a hundred or so meters—but that hundred meters mixed with a hungry alligator was just a recipe for trouble.

Trapped.

* * *

Early the next morning, Chad stood on the deck, leaning on the railing and looking out onto the lake. He'd already had a few. More than a few. A half dozen beer and around a quarter bottle of rum.

"Come on, you bleedin' bastard, show yourself!" he shouted and hurled an empty beer can at the water. "I said 'come on!'" He hurled another. As if the can hitting the surface would rouse the thing.

But what if it did?

Yesterday, eating food and playing games, Chad had been fine. Well, not fine-fine, but fine enough that losing Marley hadn't eaten away at him. But today . . . today was different. Again he saw her body in the water, the shreds of flesh, the smoky pool of blood surrounding her.

And that thing.

That thing that came and ate her.

Perhaps yesterday was about shock. Perhaps it was about denial. Perhaps it was about pretending it had all been a dream and Marley was really okay and any moment she'd come out that door, healthy as always.

But today . . . today was about reality.

Marley was gone.

He had gotten serious with her—but not *too* serious; serious enough to keep the relationship going long-term, but not serious enough to be completely devoted to her in all ways, shapes and forms. But right here, on this deck, he was devoted to her and it felt like a piece of his heart was in the water with her.

Chad's head swam from the booze and he let out a small burp. He pulled out a fresh beer from his back pocket, opened it, and took a sip. It was warm, but he didn't care. He then switched to the bottle of rum and took a swig. Then another.

"Come out of the water and fight me!" he shouted.

Small footsteps thumped on the floorboards behind him. Either Dave had learned to tippy-toe or it was Alana.

A hand grazed his shoulder then suddenly pulled back. "You should keep it down," she said.

"Why?" he replied, full volume.

"Because" —she nodded her head to the side toward the lake— "you know."

"Yeah, I know, okay, Alana!" he barked back. He guzzled his beer and nearly finished it. Another burp—a longer one—had stopped him.

"How many have you had?"

"Doesn't matter," he said. He finished the beer off and threw it good and hard against the water as if trying to sink it like a stone. The can hit then bounced up and floated along the water's surface.

Alana didn't reply but instead had this look on her face that read: Okay, fine, I'll stay out of it.

Dave poked his head out the cabin door, looked toward the mainland then in Chad's direction. He didn't say anything either then went back inside. Chad knew Dave understood. He knew he got what it was like to lose the girl you loved to a man-eating gator. Knew what it was like to see them torn open and eaten.

An engine rumbled somewhere across the way. Chad looked in its general direction and saw a single-bladed-run pontoon come gliding across the water at a good clip. It had two occupants.

Always ride in pairs, he thought absentmindedly, thinking back to the two youths in the boat.

The guys on the pontoon gave them a friendly wave.

Chad gave them the finger. He didn't even think to look at Alana's reaction.

One of the guys on the pontoon gave him the finger back. In retaliation, Chad raised both arms and gave them the bird from both hands. This time the guys on the pontoon changed course and headed toward them.

Great, Chad thought, *now look what I've done.* The guys pulled up pretty close and killed their motor. They both looked to be about in their mid-forties, classic hicks with long scraggly beards, overalls, no shirts on either, with arms as red as tomatoes.

"You got a problem there, Bubba?" one of the guys asked.

"I got lots of problems," Chad replied.

Alana pulled on his arm just above the elbow. "Chad, don't."

He tugged his arm away.

"Looks like your girlfriend there wants you to mind your manners," said the other man.

He was going to correct him and state she wasn't his girlfriend but why bother? Was none of their business.

"Just move along," Chad said.

One guy let out a loud "Ha!" before saying, "Think you owe us an apology, there, chief."

"I think I owe you a—"

Alana cut him off. "Don't."

Chad searched the deck for the gun, something to scare these guys with. He'd left it inside.

"Well?" said the guy manning the pontoon's engine.

Chad waited a moment before responding, "I'll do you one better than an apology." He gave them the finger again then added, "There's a massive gator in these waters. Watch out for him. He'd take you both out faster than you could—"

The mammoth gator soared from the water as if on command and overturned the pontoon boat. It landed on the other side with a huge splash. Chad and Alana stepped back from the railing as the two guys bobbed up to the water's surface.

"Holy hell! What was that?" one guy said.

"Mammoth gator," Chad muttered.

The guy turned his head toward him as if to ask "What?" but the moment the quizzical look crossed his face, the gator surfaced and headed toward him like a torpedo, opened its mouth, and bit straight through him. The gator's tail swooshed along the water and smacked the other guy, knocking him unconscious. He floated on the water, arms outspread. The gator spun around and swallowed him whole.

Screaming, Alana ran back toward the cabin.

His legs turning to rubber, Chad simultaneously thought to follow her and also his wish to fight the monster in the water. After a weird moment of being torn between the two, he moved to run back to the cabin.

The gator propelled itself on the deck, its giant weight crashing down and taking Chad and the decking that ran alongside the cabin down with it. Chad hit the water with a splash; his chin also smacked down on a broken piece of decking. He bit his lip and he tasted blood.

"Help!" he cried, treading water. "Help!"

The door to the cabin didn't open, and rage filled him at neither Dave nor Alana coming out running to his rescue. He glanced around. Splinters of wood floated on the water's surface. He tried to locate a sharp one, something good and thick and heavy yet pointy as hell. There was one piece, a good twenty-meter-swim away. Limbs like noodles thanks to the panic, he tried swimming toward it anyway. Perhaps he could stab the creature with it.

When he got about halfway there, there was a yank on both his legs and he was pulled beneath the surface. He tried swimming for the top but the sharp grip around his legs only grew stronger, and he knew that if he fought and swam upward any harder he'd separate his legs at the knees. Panic getting the best of him, he inhaled a lungful of dirty water. Cold filled him and on reflex he tried breathing again but to no avail.

The tug on his legs pulled him down further . . . then released. The next thing he felt was giant spikes cutting into his middle and his stomach tearing apart.

|| ||

When Dave walked into the bedroom on Alana, she stood with her arms crossed, staring out the window. He came up behind her and peered over her shoulder. The giant gator was out there on the water, the massive hump of its back partially above the surface, its enormous face and snout the same. Its almost-calculating eyes stared at them as if it was working through what its next move would be and how it would take them out.

"How long has he been like that?" Dave asked.

It took a moment for her to reply. "At least an hour. I just can't stop staring at him." She licked her lips, which Dave noticed were chapped. "He hasn't moved. At most, he dipped beneath the surface for a moment then came back up right in the same spot. He knows we're in here."

Dave didn't know much by way of gator intelligence. Like most, he thought they operated primarily on instinct, no real intellect or rational thought. This gator seemed different: a monster set apart with the ability to think. He wondered if the gator could see Alana through the window.

He put his arm around her shoulder. "Come on. Standing here's not doing any good. It'll only increase your worry."

"*My* worry?" she said. "If I turn my back on the thing, it feels like it'll suddenly spring to life and pile-drive its way through the wall and eat me."

He understood what she meant because he felt the same way. Yet he also knew standing there staring at the thing and fretting wouldn't help anything. He pulled harder on her shoulder, this time turning her to face him. Unexpectedly, she fell into his arms and started sobbing. He held her as she shook in his arms, some sobs bigger and deeper than others.

"Why is this happening?" she asked with a voice thick with tears.

He squeezed her tighter. "I don't know." He looked out the window. The gator was still there, and he imagined it knew Alana had broken down and it had finally won in terms of mentally and emotionally breaking her. Dave also knew the thing was close to finally breaking him as well.

Jessica.

Chad.

Ian.

Marley.

All dead.

Alana stopped crying and just let him hold her. Then she started up again, this time softer than the first. It didn't last as long either, and she finally stilled. She looked up at him with tear-stained eyes, a few still rolling down her cheeks. He pressed his forehead against hers and the two remained like that for a moment before his lips found hers and the two kissed. At first, it was a simple brush, then quickly grew passionate and deeper. Tongues licked the others' and then they quickly pulled apart.

"Sorry," Dave said, glancing away.

Alana sniffled. "Me, too."

"I feel bad. Jessica . . ." He looked back at her.

"I'm the same way. I guess . . . I guess things just happen. Desperation. The need for love."

It wasn't love that just happened here, but Dave understood what she meant. She was talking about connection, the compelling need to be close to someone and feel safe in the midst of chaos.

"It won't happen again," he said.

She nodded her understanding and sniffled once more. "I know. That's fine. Really, it's okay."

The two looked at each other, and for a moment he thought they'd forget what they just said and kiss again.

Instead, Alana moved back to the window and resumed the same stance as before: arms crossed, legs shoulder-width apart. Dave went beside her but this time kept a safer distance.

The gator was gone.

12

The next day, Alana stood in front of the living room window in the same pose she had back in the bedroom. Dave sat on the floor next to her, counting bullets.

"Thirty-four," he said. "That's all we got."

She barely acknowledged him but the number registered. Thirty-four chances to take the creature down if they got close enough to it. She just wasn't sure if they would—or if they did, if she even *wanted* to be that close to it. Actually, she didn't. She wanted to be as far away from the thing as possible, but the more time went on, the more the giant gator had them in its territory. The cabin had drifted a long way from shore and swimming the distance to the mainland was now impossible.

Out there, the gator was still on the water. Had been all morning.

It looked at her.

She looked at it.

Alana didn't know how long they had been playing this game of who would blink first. Every so often the gator would allow its enormous body to rise above the waterline so she could get a good look at its girth and length. Even from over here in the safety behind the window, when it showed it was the width of two adult gators and almost triple the length of the same. She shuddered. She could only imagine how much the thing needed to eat and couldn't fathom how it could even survive out here without eating the place completely empty. And where it had come from?—She didn't know. A science experiment gone wrong? A product of nature? A weird case of gigantism but in an alligator?

"What's it doing?" Dave asked.

"Same as always: staring at me," she replied.

She glanced down at Dave. He had just finished boxing the bullets. He then went and opened various parts of the rifle, presumably to check it was clean and nothing might get in the way of interfering with a shot.

"You're getting good at that," she said.

"Had to teach myself."

"Well, good job."

There was silence for a moment.

"You could almost just stand here and aim at it," she said. "Maybe get off a few shots to its head."

"Hmph. I wish," he said. "I might be able to line a couple up but I don't have steady hands . . . at least the kind required to make sure I hit it between the eyes. Thing is, it's been shot at before and it didn't seem to make a difference." He sighed. "Frankly, I think this gun is useless and it's more just to make us feel better than actually do any good. That hide that thing has, it's probably like Kevlar. At most, it probably just feels the impact of the bullet, like a sharp and targeted push. I really don't think this gun is going to do us any good."

"Then why count the bullets?"

"Inventory. Some element of control amidst the chaos." He looked up at her and his eyes read concern.

She glanced back at the gator. It was gone. "I think it went under the water."

"Could be anywhere, then," he said.

"Could be."

Dave got off the floor, made sure the rifle was loaded, then stuffed the box of bullets into his pocket. He came close to her. Too close. Their arms brushed, and even though neither was attached to each other, the warmth of his skin against hers sent a pleasant tremble throughout her body. She thought back to that kiss and wondered what it meant, then chocked it up as nothing and just a strange moment of need in a strange moment of fear.

His eyes looked into hers and for a second she thought he was going to kiss her again. His attention then raised to the window. "Oh, there he is."

She looked. The gator was back half above the water's surface. Alana thought she knew it had only one thought on its mind: how to get in and eat them. She had the creeping feeling it was only a matter of time before it'd figure out a way and kill them both.

Dave stepped away from her and paced along the walls of the room. A few times he rapped his knuckles against the drywall and stopped where the sound was less hollow.

"What you doing?" she asked.

"Getting a feel for the framing," he said. He then seemed to consider his own words. "It'd take some work and creativity, but maybe we can knock out a wall, build a second raft. It'd be bigger and stronger than the first. Could even piece together some of the framing from elsewhere in the cabin and build a makeshift paddle. Two of them, with you and I both digging hard and deep and propel this thing along as fast as possible." He rapped on the wall a couple more times. "What's he doing now?"

Alana checked. "Back under again, which is unusual. He'd been floating along the surface nearly all morning."

"Maybe he senses something."

"Yeah. Us."

"Or . . . something else."

She kept her eye on the spot where the gator had been. A few minutes later it resurfaced around twenty feet from where it usually was. She took a good look at what was around it and saw it wasn't alone.

13

Six other gators surrounded the giant one, each with their snouts just above the water's surface, pointed at the behemoth like missiles.

Dave didn't know what they had in mind.

"I should get the gun," he said.

"What for?" Alana asked.

"Those six others. Protect us. Eliminate further danger in the water."

"I don't really think that's going to be a problem," she said and pointed.

The six gators were closing in on the big one. Dave had no idea if alligators ever hunted in groups. He actually knew next to nothing about their behavior at all other than they were dangerous and killed their prey without mercy. Perhaps some sort of sixth sense was kicking in between the half dozen other killing machines. Perhaps they knew the big one was a threat both to them and to their food supply.

"They're not going to be able to do a thing to it," Dave said.

"How can you be so sure?"

"It's hide is like armor. One can only imagine how dense it is, never mind the muscle tissue underneath. Even if those other gators sunk their teeth all the way in, they won't penetrate deep enough to do any lasting damage."

"They're operating on instinct, maybe," she said.

"Probably . . . or some weird sort of reptilian intelligence. I don't know."

The first gator moved in. Judging by where its snout peeked above the waterline to where its tail did the same, Dave guessed the thing to be a dozen feet long. The gator moved in slowly, as if thinking the giant one wouldn't be able to sense its presence. The moment the smaller gator came in opening its mouth, the giant gator whipped around and bit the thing's head off as if it was nothing. Gator blood spread above the water and the headless alligator's corpse drifted away with the generated waves.

Two more gators moved in, one from either side. The giant gator spun in the water and faced the one to its left head-on. It used the whipping motion of its tail to swat the other gator away and send it tumbling atop the water's surface. The two gators squared off, the little one—yet another estimated twelve-footer—slowly opened its mouth in a display of supposed dominance. The giant gator propelled itself through the water toward it, crashing into it like a battering ram. The smaller gator's body simply floated there and Dave didn't know if the thing was dead or merely unconscious. From behind, the gator that got swatted away seemed to regroup and was joined by one other. They both closed in. The giganti-gator once more spun in the water, creating massive waves. It plowed into one and gripped it between its teeth, then tossed it up into the air and caught it in its mouth and began gulping it down whole. The other gator seemed to have seen its opening and tried taking a bite out of the giganti-gator's neck. The giant gator crashed its head down upon it, then submerged itself completely. Quickly, the gator that made the attack was sucked under the water and Dave had no doubt the thing was getting barrel-rolled across the lake's bottom.

The other alligator, the one Dave thought that might have been unconscious, came to life and disappeared under the water. The last one backed away as if in retreat. The water's surface burst open and the small alligator was slammed side-to-side as if the giant gator was using it as a baseball bat against the water's surface. It then threw the alligator up in the air and dove out of the water, catching it between its teeth and disappearing beneath the surface with it.

Blood drew to the surface, making the murky water even darker.

The giganti-gator came up halfway atop the waterline and stared the final gator down. This last small gator, Dave estimated, seemed to be about fifteen feet long, sheer muscle, and a powerhouse to be reckoned with on any other occasion.

The giant gator sped toward it, mouth open full like a wall of muscle and scales. The mouth then came snapping down, and though Dave couldn't see exactly what happened, he judged by Alana's yelp she caught a glimpse of the smaller alligator being torn in half.

The huge gator whirled around in the water, then went chomping after the bits and pieces of alligator limbs that floated on the water's surface.

Butterflies hit Dave's stomach both in awe at the display of power and also in fear. He caught his legs start to wobble beneath him, and he had to brace his footing so he wouldn't accidentally collapse.

The only sounds Alana made were a combination of heavy breathing and whispering over and over, "Oh no, oh no, oh no."

Dave took a deep breath himself and exhaled slowly. He put his arm around her and drew her in close. Alana put her head on his shoulder.

"We have to get out of here," she said. "We have to, we have to, we have to."

He gave her shoulder a squeeze. "I know," he whispered. "I just don't know how."

They both stared out onto the lake.

The giganti-gator was gone, leaving blood on the water.

Dave held her tight and she fell apart in his arms. Her sobs sent her shoulders up and down in sharp jerks.

"Shhh," he said, "it's going to be okay." *And that's totally not true. We're both going to die out here.* What if he threw Alana out into the water as bait and while the gator went to work on her he took a chance and swam for shore? It was a fleeting thought and one that made his stomach sour. *Coward.* No, he'd stand by her side until the very end.

Whatever that looked like.

The giganti-gator resurfaced, aimed at the cabin.

It swam toward them, picking up speed.

14

Alana shrieked, and a jolt of terror buzzed through her bones. Her muscles locked and it was only when Dave pulled her back from the window did her legs start to function again.

Even from where they stood, she saw the top part of the gator's maw open, its bloodstained teeth like sharp pink and red tusks. The teeth came mashing down, and even through the cabin's walls, she heard the railing and decking crunch and snap as the thing chomped its way through. A loud splash shot up and coated the window, sending all ablur. More splintering of wood and a sudden thud that shook the walls told her the gator had eaten its way right through and it'd only be a matter of moments until—

All went quiet.

Filthy water ran down the window and through the faint brown tint it left behind, the sky beyond looked clear, and for a second Alana's heart slowed as if nothing had happened.

Water.

The sound of water rushing.

Through the walls.

So loud.

So powerful.

With a sudden wham, the wall was struck and the window shattered in its frame. Bits of wood and drywall snapped inward, sending her and Dave stumbling several steps back.

"The door! The door!" Dave shouted and pulled on her hand, leading her to it.

The moment they turned for the exit, her mind filled with the image of the destroyed decking on the other side of the door and the vast expanse of muddy lake between the cabin and the mainland. Her head snapped back to see the mammoth gator come bursting through the wall, sending shards of wood and drywall hurtling in their direction. They ducked; sharp splinters grazed her skin and produced blood.

The giganti-gator whipped its head in their direction, its eyes nothing but reptilian fury, its tail snapping around with speed and taking out the load-bearing support beam that held the wall to her right in place. The wall partially collapsed. The gator opened its mouth, its jaw and teeth filling her entire field of vision.

Tears involuntarily welled in her eyes, and through the blur, the gator snapped its mouth shut, as if warning her and Dave were about to be its next meal.

Behind her, Dave fumbled with the door. She checked on his progress and couldn't figure out what was taking so long then saw his hands and arms were shaking so badly he could barely grip the knob to turn it and get them away from the monster.

Her legs suddenly gave out from the adrenaline, and she stumbled into him, knocking him away from his work.

The gun, she thought. She took a quick look around for it, then glanced back at the gator and realized those tiny .22s would do absolutely nothing to the beast.

The gator opened its mouth again and thrashed its head and tail about. Its head smashed against the wall to her left, crashing clean through to the other side and sending the roof down on its head just as its tail did the same to the wall on the right. The roof broke just above and in front of Alana and fell down on the gator; the gator fell through the flooring and into the lake beneath. She could only guess its violent movement and the weight of both it and the roof had been too much for the floor to bear.

Water sprayed up as the gator hit the lake, soaking her and Dave in a muddy deluge.

They both sputtered and gasped for air, and before she could even take a fresh lungful of oxygen, the gator surfaced and propelled itself out of the water, mouth shut, and crashed into her, taking her and it smashing into the kitchen behind. The small of her back slammed into the counter's edge, bending her in half. Something cracked loud and clear and her legs went suddenly numb and she found herself on the floor, the gator's giant head right in front of her.

Somewhere on the other side of the pain gripping her body, Dave called her name.

Called it again.

And again.

The gator opened its mouth and hurled itself toward her, its top row of teeth coming straight for her face, its bottom row for her legs and torso.

"Alana!"

"Dave!" she shouted, but she didn't know if he heard her as the gator's massive tooth cleaved her skull in half like an axe.

15

Alana's blood sprayed out on either side of the gator's mouth. The thing's body was so big it hid the rest of the carnage from Dave's view.

Heart racing, his first instinct was to run. His second instinct was to attack the monster. His third was realizing the foolishness of trying to take on the beast.

He looked to the door. It was still shut. He hadn't gotten it open in time and now Alana . . .

The gator shuffled its weight around in the kitchen's tiny space then moved with such lightning speed its enormous tail took out the cupboards and stove behind it.

It slightly opened its mouth. A chunk of Alana's face dripped off its teeth, her dead eye popping onto its tongue.

Trembling, Dave slowly backed toward the door, then found himself past it and at the shattered wall a foot beyond. He didn't need the door. But the water . . . the water was the gator's element. There was no way he could outswim it. No way he could surv—

The gator moved toward him, and Dave turned and dove off the cabin and hit the murky lake. He stayed under the water as long as he could, swimming in what he thought was the mainland's direction. His lungs ached, then pounded; they begged for air. His adrenaline-fueled limbs propelled him a little bit more forward then he broke the surface, breathing hard and deep. He'd been off in his estimate of the mainland's direction. It was at about a forty-five-degree angle to his left. He immediately turned and swam as fast as he could toward it.

It was so far away.

Bits of wood from the cabin were scattered here and there, floating on the water's surface, but none not even remotely close enough to be within reach.

The gator!

Where was it?

Dave wanted to stop and look around, see if he could see it, but instead knew any second lost could be that one second that would save his life.

He swam.

And swam.

And swam.

And no matter how hard he pushed himself through the water, the mainland didn't seem to be getting any closer.

* * *

After a while of swimming as hard and as fast as he could, Dave's muscles quit on their own, and he righted himself in the water—treading—catching his breath. How foolish: All his splishing and splashing no doubt leading the gator straight to him. Not as if the gator wasn't coming for him anyway. There was no way the beast would let him live, and there was no way the thing was full. It chomped down six alligators plus Alana . . . plus the others. And who knew what else when it hadn't been around.

The thing . . . he had only seen it in its entirety when it had come into the cabin. He glanced back over his shoulder. The cabin was far away now, probably around a couple hundred feet. He still had a couple hundred more to go if he was going to make it to land.

But that gator . . . the thing was like a dinosaur.

Was it a dinosaur? Was what everyone been told about their extinction true? Did some still lurk in the shadows whether on land or in the water? Was there some weird government conspiracy to cover it up so as to not send people into a panic?

Dave set his eyes back on the shoreline, stretched out his arms one at a time, and crawled through the water as fast as he could. Breathing heavy now, he could only exert himself in short spurts before having to tread and rest again.

Jessica.

He imagined being her, there in the water, and then suddenly seeing this giant alligator coming for her. He could only imagine staring that thing in the mouth, seeing nothing but a vacuous cave that only filled itself with flesh and blood. He could only imagine the smell, the air of decaying meat of whatever was rotting on its insides while it digested its last meal. He'd seen the monster's power; sheer, indomitable mass, muscle, and strength. Sheer size. Sheer length. Sheer girth.

A giganti-gator death machine.

He moved forward at a slow paddle, all he could muster.

Just keep moving forward, he thought. *One pull through the water at a time.* Thing was, it seemed the waves were moving in his direction and each pull forward felt like it set him two paddles back.

"Doesn't matter," he said. "Just try."

His body went hollow at the notion the giganti-gator was right behind him, and his strength waned even more. He had to look. Needed to check.

He did.

The thing wasn't far away and swam toward him.

Slowly.

16

Dave's heart galloped, and immediately his mind went to what it might feel like when the thing devoured him. He hoped it was quick. He hoped it would bite his head off or get him by the neck and make him bleed out almost instantly. Even getting a chomp to the leg and severing the femoral artery would do the trick.

The giant gator went under the water.

Dave braced himself for the bite, then adrenaline kicked in anew, and he went for the shoreline, swimming as fast as he could. This time it seemed like he was gaining distance and reveled in the feel of his body moving through the water. His muscles ached with the trembling knowledge the gator was somewhere beneath him.

Why wasn't it attacking him?

Come on, end this quick or let me get away. His eyes welled with tears, and the fear of death and what possibly awaited him on the other side took his breath away. He wasn't religious, but he didn't discount it either. Were those crazy Christians right? Was it Heaven or Hell after life on Earth? The thought of appearing before a set of golden gates temporarily put his heart at ease, then the terrifying thought of facing some horned scaly-skinned devil made of flame caused it to race again.

Wish I knew, he thought. He went under the water, muscles flat-out fatigued. He surfaced and swam slowly . . . then went under again. Beneath the murk, he envisioned the gator eyeing him from wherever it was, biding its time, taunting him with its presence.

Dave resurfaced and gasped for air.

Shore.

He had to get to shore.

To his right he noticed a small dark shape poking its scaly head just above the waterline.

Another alligator.

It swam toward him a little then disappeared beneath the surface.

Clenching his teeth and mustering all his strength, he started swimming again.

Something sharp tugged at his foot and jerked him under the water.

This was it.

Any moment now he'd be dragged under and brought to the bottom of the lake.

Another tug . . . then sharp pain cut through his ankle, and a foul yank and a sudden numbness told him the gator had torn his foot off.

Mind reeling, heart racing, his whole body shook when blood swirled to the surface in a series of smoky, inky blots.

The throbbing of his missing foot kicked in and his whole leg was on fire from the pain. He couldn't even use it to kick anymore. He tried dog-paddling for shore, using his one good leg to help him get there.

Dizzy, he went under the water when something heavy bumped both his legs. He surfaced, coughed up lake water, then floated. His breath came in short, choppy gasps.

Another sharp prick lit up where his foot had gone missing then suddenly there was a strange current under the water, the water pulling away from him. Suddenly, not far from him, the giant gator surfaced and came down with a splash, the small gator in its mouth. The resulting wave sent Dave floating quickly along the water's surface near some of the cabin's debris.

It also got him closer to shore.

He looked at the piece of wood beside him. Its end was sharp.

His ankle and leg throbbed and screamed with pain.

More blood swirled around him and a headache formed around his eyes. He lay on his back to stay afloat, his right hand gripping the sharp piece of wood that was around three feet long.

You're gonna die out here, he thought. The water just along the surface was warm.

Blood warm.

Time stopped for a moment, and it was as if there was a disconnect on his awareness because the next thing he saw was himself using the sharp end of the wood to poke a hole in his T-shirt and get a tear going on the fabric. He ripped the wet cloth as best he could then took the strip of material under the water and lifted his knee in an effort to make a tourniquet.

He went under.

He quickly came back up, the waves from the giant gator's splash still pushing him to shore.

Dave lifted his leg again and went back under, this time staying focused on tying off where his foot had been severed. He did as good as job as he could and cinched the thing tight and did a double knot. He swam for the surface, took in a big gulp of air when he broke it, then swam the few feet to the sharp shard of wood. Even though it was nothing more than a severed two-by-four, its buoyancy helped keep him afloat. Just in time, too.

The giant gator headed his way.

* * *

Dave turned to swim to shore, then turned back to see the thing's enormous head ram right into him. It kept its mouth closed, the small alligator's head and tail sticking out of either side of it. The big gator then opened its mouth then chomped down . . . but not at Dave. Instead, it went to work gulping down the other alligator.

Once more, Dave tried swimming for shore only for things to repeat themselves and the big gator ramming into him. It pushed him through the water.

As if it made its presence known of its own accord, Dave suddenly felt the two-by-four in his hand. He adjusted his grip so he could use it to stab the monster's head. He brought his hand as high out of the water as he could then stabbed the gator with the two-by-four's sharp end. It buried itself in the thing's scaly hide not even an inch. He jerked it out of the shallow hole and tried again. Same thing. He then stabbed at the monster over and over again until the sharp end of the two-by-four broke and it was useless as a weapon. Dave tried beating at the gator with the piece of wood but to no effect.

The creature gave him a final push then as Dave floated several feet away, charged right for him, mouth open. Dave swam backward and the monster's teeth mashed down on the water, its enormous mouth creating more waves on impact.

Dave looked behind him.

Land wasn't that far away.

He pulled himself through the water, trying to get to it as quickly as he could.

The gator came at him again, clearly toying with him. Its mouth opened and again Dave avoided being bitten.

Shore.

So close.

Maybe thirty feet. Forty at most.

The gator disappeared under the water.

Land.

Swim!

17

Dave went for it, pulling himself through the water with everything he had, ignoring the fiery pain in his leg and the images of him leaving an inky trail of blood through the water. He couldn't sense the gator behind him, but that didn't mean it wasn't there. This time, he didn't look back. If the monster was going to take him down, it was going to take him down and there'd be nothing he could do about it anyway. Even now, the apprehension of a giant mouth encasing his body began to ease, and he didn't know if it was delirium from the blood loss or total exhaustion causing that. Probably a combination of both. What he did know was this gator wasn't exhibiting its usual predatory behavior. If the kill was there, gators went for it, and he'd seen this monstrosity do that on more than one occasion. This time, though, it wasn't different. Perhaps the giant alligator had above-level intelligence. Perhaps it somehow knew he was the only human left and wanted to toy with him first before going in for the kill. Or, perhaps, it had finally filled its belly, and as much as it wanted to do Dave in, it couldn't and so wasn't moving in. Perhaps, even, the gator had remembered Dave being with Jessica the night of the first kill and was saving him for a savory last meal in a twisted moment of triumph.

A dozen feet from shore, Dave was finally able to put his good leg down. The water came up to his neck but his toes touched bottom. He looked over his shoulder.

The giganti-gator was out of sight.

He swam a few more feet inland then touched down again, this time his weight settling on his remaining foot. His other footless leg came down beside it and it throbbed with sharp pain. Dave went horizontal again and swam as fast as he could until he crawled on hands and knees across the remaining stretch of muddy lake bottom before finally coming onto shore. Breathing in hard and deep, a sudden sense of safety came over him, and for a half-second thought he was in the clear and could finally relax and re-group.

Water lapped against his toes and its dirty warmth got him going again. He dragged himself along the ground and crawled as fast as he could.

Forward. Forward. Forward. His only thought. His only focus.

Trees.

If he could get to the trees, he could get to his vehicle parked on the other side. He could maybe drive for help.

He could get away.

Dave scrambled himself upright, and the sudden rush of gravity seemed to pull every ounce of blood out of him from head to toe. His leg leaked red where the foot had been bitten off. He hopped on one leg, arms flailing both for balance and momentum, and headed for the trees.

That's when he heard the hiss. It hit his ears then the sound searched out his heart and made his leg give way. He fell forward, smacking his face into the ground. The dull thunk of the impact echoed in his skull.

Dave crawled forward.

The ground vibrated beneath him in heavy thrums.

He collapsed, and his heart beat so hard it hurt. Arms weak, total fatigue encompassing him, he made one last ef-fort to pull himself forward before collapsing again. Some-how, he rolled onto his back and took in the blue sky. So peaceful. A few bright cotton clouds encircled the sun.

The hiss returned, and the giganti-gator lumbered toward him. It slowly opened its mouth, then snapped it shut, the very closing of it so loud it sent a jolt through Dave's system.

In a flash, the gator lunged forward, opened its mouth, and dug its teeth and gums under Dave and began pulling him in. Dave held out his hands in a feeble effort not to go in any further.

As the gator's teeth came down across his ribs and cut him in two, the last thing Dave saw was another, even larger, giganti-gator coming out of the water.

It had to be its mother.

Giganti-gator Death Machine II

PROLOGUE

She watched as her baby swam toward the other gators invading their territory. The ten other gators should've known better, should've known they didn't stand a chance against a pair of beasts more than five times their size.

The baby moved in and immediately two of the gators swam toward it. All it took was one swirling motion in the water and the baby bit the head off one gator and struck the other with its tail. After the strike, the baby whirled around and bit off half the other gator's body.

The mother watched in pride as her baby emerged through the blood darkening the already-muddy waters and headed for the nearest gator. This one moved in with its mouth open, but its head was easily engulfed by the baby's giant maw.

Two more swam in, these two coming in from the sides. The mother was briefly tempted to interfere and rescue her baby, but instead, let her spawn handle her attackers. Another swirl and the first gator was swallowed whole. While it was being worked down the baby's throat, the baby moved in and chomped down on the other gator's tail end, removing half its body.

More blood.

The baby gulped the gators' parts back.

Five more.

One swam away, its predatory instincts seeming to fail it.

The remaining four moved in all at once. The baby bit through one straight across its middle, swimming clear through the other side. Two moved in close and the baby bit both their heads off simultaneously.

More blood.

Darker water.

One more gator.

This final one opened and closed its mouth several times, then charged the baby, mouth open, teeth showing as if in feral pride. The baby met it head on, mouth closed, and let the remaining gator get a nip in on her snout as if toying with it. She rammed the little gator and shoved it back through the water before swimming at it full force, mouth open. She scooped the entire gator into her mouth and processed her kill.

Once more, the baby emerged through the blood and joined its mother.

Food supply was getting low here.

It was time to move on to better waters.

I

"This is stupid," Billy said.

"What?" Bill senior asked.

"I'm on water skis. On a dock."

"Learn the proper form first then you can go in the water," Bill said. He handed his son the handle, which was attached to the rope that was hooked up to the boat not far from the dock. His wife, Wilma, and other son, Bart, were in the boat. Wilma waved. Bill waved back. "Just give us a couple more minutes," he told her. She waved her acknowledgement.

"How come Bart doesn't have to do this?" Billy asked.

"Because he's ten and you're twelve and he's water-skied before."

"This is stupid."

"You already said that." He adjusted Billy's hands on the handle then stood beside him. "Now bend your legs slightly. Try and do this straight-legged and you'll fall in the water."

Billy sighed and mimicked his father. "There, see? I can do it."

Bill inspected him. His son's form wasn't bad. "Okay, now let's go in the water." He helped his son into the lake, skis and all, and got him set up behind the boat. "When the boat pulls you, you have to lean back or it'll yank you forward. Likewise, when you begin to rise up, you got stand hard so you're upright or, again, it'll jerk you forward and you'll fall."

"Yeah, yeah. I've seen people do it. I'll be fine."

Bill got in behind Billy and adjusted him in the water into the proper position. "I'll stay here for the first round then get in the boat before you go around again. Know what to do when the boat stops?"

"You told me a thousand times: let go of the rope."

"Right. Let go of the rope and eventually you'll sort of sink-ski back into the water."

"Then get eaten by a shark. Better, an alligator."

Bill shook his head. "There are no alligators in these waters. This is a lake. Alligators live in swamps and stuff."

"Whatever you say."

"Where'd you get the idea there were alligators here?"

Billy fidgeted with the rope's handle. "TV. Alligators live in water and this is water we're in."

"There are no alligators out here in Lake Machaka."

"Darn."

"Or sharks."

"Double darn."

"Okay, let's give this a go." Bill waved to Wilma in the boat and gave her a thumbs up. She nodded then got to work getting the boat going. The boat started with a roar and she slowly moved forward, pulling the rope taught. Bill noticed his son's hands tighten their grip on the handle. "You got this, junior. You got this."

The boat went loud and started forward with a jerk. Soon, Billy was out of the water, hanging on for dear life. He wobbled forward and backward and Bill was sure his kid would fall face-first into the lake. Somehow, Billy was able to right himself and maintain his balance.

The kid got it on his first try. Not bad at all. Most people fell over the first time they tried skiing.

Bill treaded water by the dock while Wilma took their son for a short jaunt around the lake. They agreed she wasn't going to take him too far. Just a short ride so he could get the hang of it first. Bill watched with pride as his son—all ridged and taught—kept his balance and stayed within the wake.

Something beneath the water brushed by Bill's feet. Something rough. Must've been a sharp fish fin or something. The quick image of a shark went through his mind's eye, but then thought that was ridiculous. It was probably just a fish with rough scales that brushed against him at just the right angle. Nothing to worry about.

Wilma rounded back to the dock and Billy let go of the rope. He stayed above water for a few seconds before slowly sinking back into it then tumbled backwards after his balance gave way.

Bill chuckled. "How was it?" he shouted above the boat's motor. Wilma was turning back.

"Awesome!" Billy said.

"Good. Let's get ready for round two."

* * *

"Do you think he'll manage?" Wilma asked.

Bill was now in the boat and eyeing his son, who was in the water and in the ready position behind them. "He already did your little circle once no problem. Doing the lake, or a good chunk of it, shouldn't be an issue."

"I just worry for him. He's so little."

"Would you cut it out? He'll be fine."

"Come on, let's go," Bart said.

"Dad!" Billy called from behind.

Bill gave him a wave. "Yeah, yeah. Hit it, Wilma."

She turned in her seat and gave Billy a thumbs up. He returned the gesture. "Let's hit it, then." She gunned the motor and the boat lurched ahead, yanking Billy from the water. He teetered forward a bit then regained his balance and hung on with a huge smile on his face.

"Yay! Keep it up!" Bart shouted, hands cupped around his mouth.

Billy just smiled big and wide.

Bill checked up on him. The boy was a natural. He remembered when he first learned how to waterski and it took a half a dozen tries before he was able to stand up and ride the wake. He thought about telling Billy to try and ski outside it where the water was smoother, but he also didn't want to send him for a tumble. Better let him just do what he was doing and build his confidence first.

Bart had his eyes off to somewhere beside the boat. Bill followed his line of sight. What was he looking at? The action was behind the boat. Bill glanced back at Billy, who was now experimenting with using one hand and then the other. Bill raised his fists together, hoping his kid would get the idea to use both hands. Billy didn't seem to acknowledge and just kept doing what he was doing.

Wilma had her eyes forward. "Bart, your brother's back there."

"He always gets all the attention," Bart said.

Bill kept an eye on his son but out of his peripheral noticed Bart wasn't watching. Not that he had to but two sets of eyes on the skier were better than one. Safety first, and all that.

"Hey," Bill said with a swat to Bart's shoulder. "What's up?"

Bart pointed. "The water's darker over there."

Bill followed his finger. It was a shadow beneath the water where it didn't belong. "Probably some weird angle of the sun."

Billy kept skiing; his father watched with pride.

"You're up next, Bart," Wilma said. "Bart?"

Bart still had his eyes on the water.

"Bart!"

Bart suddenly stood up in his seat. "Billy, look out!"

Bill turned his attention to him and yanked him back down in his chair. "Sit. Down."

He turned back to check on junior.

Billy was gone.

2

"You guys are a bloody joke." Bill looked the RCMP officer square in the eye.

"I'm sorry, sir, but Cedarhaven isn't equipped with what you're asking," the officer said. He was young and clearly naive to such a tragedy.

"My son is missing." Bill overheard Wilma and Bart crying in the cabin's kitchen. "You hear that?"

The officer cocked his head.

"That's the sound of a terrified mother and a scared kid. Now do your job and comb the lake or search the shores or do whatever it is you do when someone goes missing in the water."

"We'll do all we can, sir," the officer said. "I'm sorry for your loss."

"Loss? You bastard. My son's missing. Not dead."

"I-I'm sorry, I—"

"Get the hell out of here and do something."

The officer bowed his way out of the doorway. "We'll do what we can."

"You better or I'll kick your ass back to Winnipeg."

"Bill!" Wilma said, suddenly behind him. She had a knack for always being quiet.

The officer gave Bill a sharp look then got back in his car, flicked on the headlights, then backed out of the gravel driveway.

"You don't threaten the police," Wilma said.

"They're not cops."

"Yes, they are. Out here they are. Let them do their job."

He embraced her and she immediately broke down against his shoulder. Bill did all he could to bite back his own tears. He had to be strong. He was the leader of the home, the pillar of strength.

He could fall apart later.

Bart appeared in the landing doorway, his black hair a tussle, his hair reminding Bill of Billy's black hair. It was too painful to look at even his other son.

"Are they gonna catch the dinosaur?" Bart asked.

Bill sighed. Ever since they got off the lake after circling it over and over for any sign of Billy, Bart insisted it was a dinosaur that snatched his brother and took him underwater. "There's no dinosaur, Bart. Dinosaurs don't exist."

"They do. And one got Billy." Bart's face scrunched into a pinch. "It killed my brother!" He ran off, wailing. Bill listened to his footfalls and knew his son had run into his room. The door slam that followed confirmed it.

"You're going to need to talk to him," Bill told his wife.

"You should. You're his father."

"But you're so much gentler than I. He needs his mother's touch. Besides, I'm too pissed off to be of any use to him right now." He let her go and grabbed his jacket off the hook by the door.

"Where're you going?"

He slid his arms into the sleeves. "To find my son." He reached up into the closet across from the door and fumbled around looking for the flashlight.

"It's too dark."

"Shut it, Wilma. My kid's out there. Alive or . . . dead. Either way, he needs to be found." The thought of Billy lost in the woods rimming the other side of the lake made his heart ache.

Tears welled in his wife's eyes and he knew it wasn't from Billy's absence.

"I'm sorry," he said. "I shouldn't have snapped like that."

"No," she said, "you shouldn't have." She crossed her arms and walked away.

Bill looked to the ceiling. "Cut me a break." He didn't know if God on the other side heard him. How could God even let this happen?

Bill left the cabin and muttered, "Dinosaurs. As if."

* * *

"Ugh, dammit!" Bill said as he stumbled in the dark along the lake's edge. The light from the flashlight went this way and that until he righted himself after tripping over a tree root. He shone the flashlight in every direction he could, especially in the dark spots where the shadows were thickest by the trees. Every so often he'd see this phantom image of Billy laying there, his young body water-logged and covered in cuts and bruises. Every so often he thought he'd heard the tiny cough of a boy sputtering up water.

Get it out of your head, man, Bill thought. Even at forty-two, sometimes his imagination got the best of him.

He kept up along the bank and finally stopped after he realized he was wheezing. "Not as young as I used to be." He glanced up and shone the light far down the bank. The thing went on forever. It'd take him until tomorrow night or longer to comb the whole thing, but if the damn "cops" wouldn't do their job and find his kid, he damn well would.

He kept going, shining the flashlight every which way. He should've called in a search party. Should've called Theodore down the road. Even Marvin. Could've covered more ground. He stopped and patted his jacket for his cell-phone.

"Crap," he said. He'd forgotten that, too, in the rush to get out. "Totally alone." He took in a deep breath. "Billy!" He sucked in another lungful of air. "Billy!" His voice echoed across the lake beside him.

A low growl returned his call.

"And now there's a bear out there." He checked his jacket again for any mace. Of course. That was at the cabin, too. "One kid eaten by a dinosaur, the old man taken out by a bear. Somehow that makes perfect sense."

He shook his head at the idiotic joke and kept on.

He shone the flashlight across the water, for some reason expecting his son to be swimming across the lake toward him. It was just too dark and the flashlight's beam didn't reach all that far. "Billy! Billy, it's Dad! Where are you?"

His face cracked and the tears gushed out. "Oh God. Please. I beg You. Cut me some slack. Find my kid. Take me to him. Something. Anything. I beg You." He sniffled and wiped his eyes and nose with his sleeve. "Billy! Junior!"

There was that growl again, low and guttural. That was no bear.

It had come from the side. Bill turned and shone the light in the sound's direction.

A dinosaur stared back.

"You got to be kidd—" He looked closer. It wasn't a dinosaur. It was an alligator, and despite how low the thing seemed to try and keep itself to the ground, it was so enormous it might as well be a dinosaur.

Fear froze his heart. Instinctively, he tried to back away. His foot slipped out from under him and he dropped to his butt. Dropped the flashlight, too. When he picked it back up again and shone it at the creature, the thing was moving toward him.

Slowly.

Deliberately.

Bill scrambled back in a reverse crab-walk. He tumbled back when he hit the waterline.

The dinosaur—the alligator—moved in and rammed right up against him, shoving him a dozen feet from shore in a splash. The shock of the cold water jolted him. The gator slid into the water, its gigantic body—at least sixty feet long and ten feet wide; it was too dark to tell—bringing a mini tidal wave with it.

A second later, a giant mouth opened before him, teeth

the size of his hands and as sharp as axes already coming down on top of his body. The thing bit him in half and he felt the rushing warmth of blood escape him from the waist. His head swooned and his eyes began to close. A moment later, those axe-like teeth began to chew.

3

Wilma awoke and took in the empty spot in bed next to her. She bolted upright. "Bill!"

She jumped out of bed, threw on her robe, and scrambled down the hallway to the front room, her bare feet slapping against the wooden floor. Instead of maybe finding her husband crashed on the couch, she saw Bart tangled up in a blanket, fast asleep.

"Bill?" she whispered.

She searched every room then went outside onto the deck. She checked the parking pad. The SUV was still there. She ran up to it, thinking maybe he had used it then fallen asleep in the driver's seat after pulling up. The SUV was empty. She ran back to the cabin and headed straight for the phone. She called Bill's cell and heard its ring in the other room. He'd forgotten it.

"Where is he?" she said, turning the cordless phone off. "Dammit, Bill."

A knock at the door.

Her eyes widened. Yes!

She ran into the landing and opened the door. It was the same RCMP officer as before, a solemn look on his face.

* * *

"You look pretty loaded up there, Bart," Theodore said, admiring the multiple Nerf guns the boy had lined his body with like the Punisher.

"There's a dinosaur out there. It . . . it ate my brother, so I'm going to go kill it."

Theodore's heart sank. Wilma had dropped Bart off, them being their nearest neighbor, when the RCMP arrived with news of a body found and she had gone with the officer. Theodore didn't know the details. All Wilma said between sobs was simply, "Watch Bart. Please. I got to . . . I got to go."

Theodore hoped Bill was all right. Bill junior, too.

"I don't think there are any dinosaurs out there," he told Bart, "but if you want to go hunting you can do it in here or outside. Just stay within eyeshot of the cabin, if you do."

Bart cocked his Nerf gun. "I'll call after it's dead. You can help me drag it here so my dad can see I wasn't lying."

"He thought you were lying?" About the dinosaur, sure, all make-believe. Theodore wasn't sure where he was going with this.

"My brother was water-skiing and a dinosaur jumped out of the water and ate him. No one believes me. I'm gonna go find the dinosaur and prove it."

It was impossible to tell if the boy was telling the truth or not. Rather, if he was telling the truth of his imagination or actually believed what he was saying.

"Just stay close to the cabin. Don't go too far."

"I won't." Bart headed for the door. "I'm gonna kill that bastard."

Theodore didn't bother saying anything about the kid's choice of word.

* * *

The RCMP officer—whom Wilma finally found out was called Sal—took her to a back room in the RCMP building the next town over. It wasn't quite a morgue and wasn't quite a hospital room either. It looked like a small, barren classroom with a gurney in the middle and a small kitchenette lining the back wall. No stove or anything, but a white counter with white cupboards above it. A light blue hospital blanket—the kind used for surgery—covered a lump on the gurney.

She looked at the officer. He stared back with compassion.

"I'm going to need you to ID the body," he said.

"Body?"

He went over to the gurney and tugged at the corner of the blanket. She drew close. When he pulled the blanket away—it wasn't a body. It was parts of one. A mash of pink flesh and blue jeans and, next to it, an arm wearing the same sleeve as Bill's jacket.

Wilma collapsed to her knees. The cracked wail that sounded from her lips brought Sal down to his knees beside her to hold her close.

4

"So what did she say?" Halberto asked.

"Say what?" his brother, Alestro, replied.

They were gutting fish in the fish shack by the lake.

"When you said you wanted to round third?" Halberto had that stupid smile on his face as he cut into the fish's belly. They had a pile of six of them on the table. When you were fraternal twins at fifteen and all mama wanted to do was sit in the cabin and feed you, what else were you going to do but fish? Then again, fish was food.

"Catch me something big and fat," she had told them when they left for the docks that morning.

They hoped these jacks would suffice. Mama made a mean *casserula di pesce*.

"Jeanine told me to go to hell and stay there," Alestro said. "But she had that warm smile on her face when she said it, so I don't know." He thought of his girl back in the city. Jeanine. All brown hair with matching eyes that sucked you right in. *Damn. I'm such a sap.*

"Don't worry, you'll get her," Halberto said.

"You're a douche. 'I'll get her,' he says. You got to romance her, man. Wine and dine and stuff her with lasagna. That's how it's done. You don't just flat-out ask. Last time I take your advice."

"You're mixing men and women, there. The way to a man's heart is through his stomach. Romance is for the women, or so you say. I don't know, dude. I just ask and I just get."

"Lucky you."

"You better believe it, bro. This one chick—"

"Stop. I don't want to imagine you mackin' on some girl."

"We're twins, dude. What you got, I got. Well, my linguini is fatter."

"I'm like a lasagna noodle."

Halberto finished his gutting and slapped the fish down on the pile. "How many more do we got?"

"Um . . ." Alestro checked. "Three."

"I hate this part. Smells like *merda* in here."

"You smell like *merda*"

"Takes one to know one."

They finished up and stuffed their now-clean catch into a garbage bag.

"I'm gonna take these down to the lake for a rinse," Alestro said.

"Yeah, you do that. I'm gonna text Jeanine while you're gone and ask about your lasagna noodle."

"Douche bag."

"Mama's boy."

Alestro left while his brother got to work clearing down the table. It'd only take a few minutes to rinse the remaining guts off the fish then they'd head back to see what their mama thought. Or Halberto would insist they take a quick drive down the road to the beach to take in the girls. With the way his heart ached for Jeanine, Alestro wouldn't mind the distraction, if he was to be honest.

He went out to the water and noticed a shadowy area near its surface.

* * *

"No one ever believes me," Bart muttered as he trudged his way in between the trees that surrounded Theodore's property. He had his Nerf rifle at the ready. "There really was a dinosaur. I saw it."

He thought of Billy and how the creature dove out of the water and grabbed his brother in its mouth. He hoped Billy escaped. His brother was strong and if anyone could get away from a dinosaur, it was him.

Bart scanned the trees. Not far from him a cluster of oaks with dark bark briefly made him think he found what he was looking for but when he got closer his heart sank at it, in fact, being nothing but a couple trees that half melded together over the years.

Okay, let's think, he thought. Dinosaurs were tall so if he was going to spot one, he'd have to look up. Bart raised his gaze and searched the surrounding tree line. He looked at the branches and peered just past them in between the limbs in case the dinosaur was using the trees as cover. The dinosaur's hide and the tree bark looked similar, so he'd have to be extra careful when taking a look to make sure he didn't miss it.

He kept going: checking trees, searching high and low. He stopped walking the second a large form appeared beside him. He spun on his heels to face it and fired off every shot in the rifle.

"Ha ha! Got ya," he said then smiled. He took a step toward his target, which hadn't moved. "Dang," he said. It was just another cluster of trees. Some of his Nerf bullets were on the ground in front of it; others had gone missing in the bush.

Leaves rustled behind him and the crunching of footfalls on the dry ground rose in volume. Right then his heart galloped.

"Clever girl," he said, echoing a famous movie reference. He turned around to see the dinosaur standing before him.

This was no velociraptor nor a T-rex nor any dino he could label.

This was something different.

Something familiar.

Something he knew.

An alligator.

The thing's cold eyes bore into him. Summoning his

courage, he fired off the last few shots in the rifle right at the thing's giant head. The bullets bounced off the gator's snout. Bart dropped the rifle and pulled both handheld Nerfs from their holsters at his sides and fired away. The bullets struck their target and didn't do any damage.

The creature didn't take its eyes off of him.

Bart looked at his guns and it was then he crossed from being a child into a teen. Nerfs were for kids. Real guns were for monsters.

Like the monster in front of him.

With a shout, Bart turned tail and sprinted through the bush back to Theodore's place. He didn't look over his shoulder to see if the monster followed.

* * *

At the lake, Alestro finished cleaning the fish in the water. He brought one to his nose and took in its fishy scent. Once gutted, they didn't smell so bad. He could hardly wait for Mama to work her magic and put the *casserula* together.

After putting the fish back in the bag, a splash on the water drew his attention to the lake. He thought maybe Halberto had skipped a stone and was just playing with him.

The giant reptile moving toward him proved him wrong.

Alestro bolted upright, dropping the bag of fish. He turned heel and started running toward the fish shack. "Halberto! Alligator! Giant! Run!"

His brother didn't come out of the shack.

"Halberto!" Behind him, he heard the mammoth gator swish its way out of the water and its thumping footfalls on land. *I'm dead! I'm dead! I'm dead!*

He quickly scanned up and down the shoreline, hoping against hope someone was witnessing what was going on. There was nobody.

"Help! Halberto, help!"

His stupid brother remained in the shack. Was he even in there or did he take off without him?

The guttural growl of the gator at his heels forced him to dig in deeper and run like hell. He felt the thing's breath against his calves. Already, his thighs were turning to rubber from the exertion and the adrenaline.

"Halbert—" His feet were suddenly swept out from underneath him and he fell face-first against the grass just beside the shack. His chin hit the ground with a dull thwump, slamming his teeth together and biting off the tip of his tongue. Blood gushed from between his lips and ran down his chin. The pain brought tears to his eyes. The crunch of bone as his feet were swallowed by the beast sent a shockwave of pain up his legs. Alestro clawed at the grass in front of him, trying to pull himself forward and out of the gator's reach. The alligator could easily swallow him whole but instead worked its way up his body like a python slowly gorging on its latest prey. A warm tidal wave of blood splashed over his hamstrings and buttocks as the thing bit into him. He tried screaming his brother's name but could only cough up blood. Still, he pulled, images of Jeanine suddenly filling his mind's eye. If he could make it, if just for her, if somehow . . .

His lower back cracked as the teeth came down and all sensation escaped whatever might've been left of his legs. Agony tore into his shoulder blade muscles and his neck pounded. The creature worked its way up and his arms went numb. He couldn't even turn himself over if he wanted to to look his killer in the eye.

Alestro hacked out gobs of blood and whatever liquid that was in his stomach, staining the grass in his field of vision an awful crimson like some twisted Christmas mosaic.

Face down now, full shock erasing all pain, the last he heard was the gator's body moving along the grass as it finished its meal. And a voice: "Alestro?"

* * *

Bart tore through the forest, aiming straight for Theodore's cabin. The sound of branches breaking and parting leaves forced a screech from deep within his throat.

The cabin was in eyeshot now.

Theodore stepped out onto the porch. "Bart? What's wrong?"

"A d-dinosaur! I mean a . . . a . . . alligator. Huge. Dino-huge. Help!"

Theodore put his hands on his hips. "What are you talking abo—" His eyes went wide. Obviously he saw the beast right behind Bart. "Get inside, kid, get inside!"

The second Bart reached him, he ushered the boy inside so hard he inadvertently threw him to the floor. Theodore slammed the door closed and bolted every lock there was to bolt, which was strange because out here no one locked their doors. Why Theodore had so many . . .

"Go, go. Far side. We'll go by the patio doors. Get ready to run." Theodore was already out of breath and Bart couldn't figure out why. The old man hadn't run other than to get him inside the cabin.

The entire place shook and Bart imagined the terror outside slamming itself up against the door. He clung to Theodore with everything he had. Strong fingers clung to him as well.

"Ow," Bart said. Theodore didn't seem to have heard him. Instead, after the next cabin-shaking thunk, he dug his old fingers into him even harder. "You're hurting me."

Theodore eased up.

The place shook a third time and the door flew from its hinges, cracking in two, revealing the monster beyond. The thing was so big it couldn't fit through the door and so it backed up then lunged at the doorframe. The thing cracked with the first effort. It was old, wooden, not made of metal like the door to Bart's house back home.

The gator backed up again then drove itself through the frame and crashed through the table and chairs in its way to get to them.

Theodore's grip tightened, crushing Bart's shoulders. Then the old man collapsed, taking Bart to the ground with him.

"Theodore!" Bart pried at the man's hands as the gator

charged toward them. He got loose just as the gator opened its mouth and swallowed Theodore in one bite.

Bart scrambled past the gator, which quickly spun around and missed him with a nip. The sound of those giant teeth slamming together sent Bart's heart into overdrive. He guessed that's what had happened to Theodore: a heart attack. That's why the old man fell.

Bart escaped through the destroyed door and headed off down the road, the thundering footfalls of the gigantic gator right behind him.

5

Halberto stood there, mouth hanging open. Hot piss ran down his right leg. He got there just as his brother's head had been engulfed by this . . . this . . . giant alligator. His lower lip moved up and down on its own accord. There were words there—both English and Italian—but they wouldn't come out.

His feet wouldn't move and turned as heavy as cement blocks the moment the gator set its gaze on him.

Shaking, he tried to turn—move—run . . . but was stuck. What the hell was the matter with his legs?

A fresh discharge of urine ran the same trail as the one previous.

The gator stomped toward him, its size growing with each step forward. For a second, the reptile stopped its advance and angled its snout toward the fish shack.

Please go in there, please go in there, Halberto thought. *Maybe the stink of the fish caught its attention.*

Nope.

The gator looked at him again.

It came at him full boar.

Halberto stumbled backward, his heart elated at his ability to move, then suddenly plunking into his stomach when he fell backward. He tried crawling away, but again found himself frozen.

Terror.

Pure, unholy, pulse-pounding fear.

The gator appeared as if it could somehow gallop at him like a wild horse and he wasn't sure if it was his imagination or not. A giant, scaly foot plowed down upon his chest, crushing his ribcage. Bones snapped and he felt his guts split his sides and gush onto the grass. His head went fuzzy.

He should be dead.

He should be so dead.

Perhaps the adrenaline was keeping him going longer than he should have.

Perhaps he was somehow superhuman.

Perhaps . . .

Teeth.

* * *

Bart tore off down the road. "Mooom!"

Was he even headed the right way?

He fought back the tears. Billy. The dinos—alligator. Billy. His dad. Where was his dad?

The gator.

Billy.

Dad.

Where was his mom?

Tears ran from his eyes and snot oozed from his nose. His head swam and a headache set in. The deep banging of reptile feet behind him propelled him to run faster.

He was such a good runner. It was his favorite thing. Even played soccer back home solely because it enabled him to run-run-run. Yeah. That's it. He imagined himself on the soccer field, giving it all he had. If he could just make it to the other end where his parents were, he'd be safe. The big bad player behind him wouldn't be able to hurt him or scare him anymore.

Bart gave it all he had.

A car came down the road.

* * *

Wilma gasped. "That's Bart! Sal, slow down."

No sooner did Sal slow down the RCMP car did a—dinosaur?—appear behind Bart, chasing him down the road.

"Scratch that. Speed up," Wilma said. "Get my boy!"

Sal hit the gas hard, sped, then came to a screeching halt beside Bart. Wilma threw open her door. "Get in, get in!" She yanked Bart in by the arm and Sal spun the vehicle around while Wilma scrambled to close the door. A big bang hit the trunk when the dinosaur butted into it. A second later, metal crunched and Wilma looked over her shoulder. The thing had the car in its mouth.

"Floor it!" she shouted at Sal.

"I'm trying," he said.

The sound of tires whirring on gravel told her he had the pedal pressed flat. Dust and gravel kicked up behind him, cloaking the dinosaur in smoky dirt.

"See?" Bart said, catching his breath. "I wasn't lying. But it's not a dinosaur. It's an alligator."

"There's no such thing as an alligator that big," Sal said. He started spinning the steering wheel left then right, maybe hoping to twist the car free from the creature's grasp.

"Tell that to the thing behind us," Wilma said. She furrowed her brow. "Where's Theodore?"

"Dead. I think. Heart attack, then that thing ate him," Bart said.

Oh no, she thought. "Was Jill and Sandy home? I mean, did they get back?" Not even sure if they had come out this weekend. Jill was Theodore's wife, Sandy their kid, who was fourteen.

"No. And no Sammy either." Sammy was their Golden Retriever.

The car lurched forward when it broke free, spun its wheels for a second on the gravel road, then lurched forward again as it got traction and sped away. Wilma peered through the back window, but all the dust shrouded the creature. "Drive, drive, drive," she said.

"That's what I'm doing," Sal said.

Dinosaurs. No, wait. Alligators. Her eyes went wide. Bill. Then her son: Billy.

She clung to Bart as tight as she could as if to shield him from the monstrosity somewhere behind them.

"Where are we going?" Sal asked.

"I don't know. Just . . . away," she said.

6

Sal took them down the gravel road as fast as he could. A few times the car swerved from catching on a few trenches in the gravel. "What was that thing?" he said.

"A dino—an alligator," Bart said. "A big one."

"Impossible. Alligators don't live in these waters. They're swamp creatures, down south and all that. This is a lake."

"Well, it's here."

"But how did it get here?" Wilma asked. She could only suppose something so huge could have the leg span to eventually walk where it could and get water on its way as well. She didn't know much about reptiles or even if they—namely alligators—had to stay in a certain kind of water. All she knew was she just saw a giant one and it nearly ate the car.

Sal reached for the car's radio, presumably to call in what he'd just seen.

"We should tell people," Wilma said.

"That's what I'm doing," he replied.

She drew her attention from his hands when Bart said, "Uh, guys?" and pointed up ahead.

An enormous gator blocked the road. It wasn't facing them directly, but was angled enough that its attention would be—It set its gaze on them.

"There's two of them?" Sal said, slamming on the

brakes.

"Unless that thing can run real fast, um, yeah," Wilma said. "And this one's bigger, I think."

Sal swore then looked up at the rearview mirror then craned his neck all the way around to look out the back window.

"Don't see nothing," Bart said, looking out the rear window, too.

"Yet," Sal added.

Wilma's stomach squirmed. Two possible gators.

Two possible gigantic gators.

One on either end of them.

They were trapped.

The gator in front of them moved toward them, its pace careful and sure, as if testing the car like it would test another of its prey.

On either side of the road was a ditch. Wilma supposed it was drivable if—

Sal gunned it, heading straight for the gator.

Bart screeched in his seat.

"What are you doing?" she screamed.

Sal's eyes were deadset on the gator in front of them. "Playing chicken."

"You're so gonna lose," Bart said.

"Watch this, kid."

Just before he'd crash into the gator, Sal veered to the left and hit the ditch. In a blur of dark green scale, the gator whipped its head around and snapped at the car, catching the driver's side door in its teeth. When it jerked its head back around, it took the door off the hinges, the force also pulling the car back onto the road.

Sal cussed again, then put his foot down hard on the gas. He also fumbled around between the seats.

"Whatchya need?" Wilma asked.

"Gun. Rifle. Gun," he said.

"Road!" Wilma said, pointing ahead.

They were heading straight to the right into the trees beyond. Sal yanked on the wheel, straightening it. Just then the butt end of the car got slammed and as it spun around like a top; Wilma saw the gator had used its tail against them.

"Turn into the spin!" she told Sal, who was doing the opposite.

He hit the brakes—probably on instinct—to slow them down.

When the car finally stopped spinning, the gator's giant head was at his door. It shoved its snout into the opening and ripped him from his seat, the seatbelt cutting through him like a string through butter. Sal was pulled onto the road, the left side of his body in the creature's mouth, the rest of him torn open and dripping blood.

The car moved forward with Sal's weight off the brakes.

Bart screamed.

Wilma leaned over to cover his eyes but couldn't help but watch as the gator shifted its mouth and got the rest of Sal inside of it.

"Mommy, save me!" Bart cried.

Tears in her own eyes, she shuffled over into the driver's seat and took control of the wheel. As fast as she safely could, she did a U-turn on the road and drove past the enormous gator, which was still chewing on Sal.

"Home. I wanna go home!" Bart's eyes were red and swollen. "Let's go get Dad and go home." He sniffled.

"Bart" —she tried to look at him with compassion but had to be careful about not taking her eyes off the road— "About your father . . ."

7

Jill drove her and Sandy back from the Cedarhaven grocery store. She looked at her teenage daughter, who gazed out the window.

"Well, that was boring," Sandy said. Just then Sammy, their Golden Retriever, peeked in between the seats and tried forcing his way to the front. She shoved him back. "No." Sammy tried again and this time Sandy met him with more force. "Cut it out!"

"Don't take your frustrations out on the dog," Jill said.

Sandy shot her a scowl then rolled her eyes.

"Roll those back any further and they'll get stuck like that."

"That's what you told me when I was four and I've been doing it ever since, so, ha."

"Yeah. Ha."

"Can't believe you made me keep my cell at home. The cabin. Whatever."

"You need to get your eyes off that little screen and experience the real world."

"Like go grocery shopping in a small town?"

"Like go grocery shopping in a small town. You'll thank me one day."

Sandy raised her hand and shooed off the comment. "Whatever."

A car was driving toward them up ahead. A moment

later, Jill noticed it was RCMP. The closer they got, the more she saw something was wrong with the vehicle and it kind of clunked down the road instead of smoothly sailing along the gravel. There was motion behind the windshield.

"What's going—" She pressed her lips together when the RCMP car moved into their lane and headed right at them.

Jill hit the brakes and waited for the cruiser to come to a stop just in front of them. Was that . . . "Wilma?"

Wilma maneuvered the car right beside them, her arm moving in circles in what Jill guessed was an effort to get her to roll her window down. The cruiser car had the driver-side door missing.

"Wilma, what the hell happened?"

"Go back. Go back!" Wilma doubled over, as if saying the words had taken everything out of her.

"What happened? What's wrong?"

Wilma straightened in her seat and Bart leaned past her and said, "A massive alligator is eating everybody!"

Jill furrowed her brow and Sandy burst out laughing.

"Not kidding. It's true. Two of them!" Bart said.

Wilma still seemed to be in a state of catching her breath and simply nodded.

"What?" Jill said. "Are you serious?"

She nodded some more, then, "Yes. I don't know how. I don't know what. Two . . . huge . . . alligators. Eating. People."

"Over there?" Sandy pointed up the road.

"It ate Theodore!" Bart blurted.

"Shut up!" Wilma snapped at him.

"Theodore?" Jill said.

"Dad?" Sandy said.

"Go back. Please. Just. Go. Back," Wilma said. "Head to town. Warn everybody. It got my . . . it ate my . . . oh Bill." She broke down. Bart reached around her in a hug.

Tears pooled in Jill's eyes. Theodore. She looked to Sandy, whose lower lip trembled. Sammy pushed his way between the seats and this time Sandy didn't shoo him away.

110

Not Theodore.

Alligators?

Two of them?

Big ones?

It couldn't be. They must be mistaken. But Theodore . . .

She had to see. No. Not him.

Sandy clung to Sammy good and tight.

"We need to go," Wilma said, suddenly composed.

Jill stared at her for a while then grit her teeth. Something wasn't right. Wilma was crazy. Then again, she was in an RCMP vehicle with the door missing. Still.

She's lost it, Jill thought. *But if she's right . . . or, at least, something's happened to my hubby . . .*

She hit the gas and sped down the road, heading for her cabin.

* * *

"No, don't!" Wilma shouted after her.

"Why did she do that, Mom?" Bart asked.

She shook her head. "I don't know. All I know is I need to get you to safety and we need to tell people."

Bart settled himself in his seat. He started to cry but quickly wiped the tears and sniffled everything back.

He's trying to be brave, Wilma thought. *My poor boy. Trying to be brave for his mama.* He shouldn't have to. Shouldn't need to. She was the one who was supposed to be brave despite falling apart inside. She was the one who was supposed to comfort him. *Can't dwell on it right now. Just take what you can get and get the job done.*

They headed for Cedarhaven.

How she'd tell people about two giant alligators on a rampage, she had no idea.

* * *

Jill peeled into the parking spot by their cabin, burst out of the car and ran for the door, then stopped short when she saw the whole entrance had been destroyed.

"Theodore!" she shouted and ran inside.

"Mom!" Sandy called after her.

Blood spattered the dismantled living room.

A bark followed by a squeak from Sammy as she covered her mouth.

Sandy broke down and cried. "Dad . . ."

Jill's legs wobbled then gave out beneath her. She crawled over to her daughter and the two held each other and wept.

A low, guttural rumble sounded from outside.

Then another.

8

Jill fought the urge to move and see what was just outside their door. The moment she shifted, Sandy clung to her even tighter.

"What is it?" Sandy asked, fear coating her voice.

"Maybe just a bear."

"Or two."

Alligators, Jill thought. *No. Not here. Can't be.*

The low guttural rumblings started again . . . then movement outside. Sammy barked and cautiously approached the hole in the wall that used to be their front door.

"Sammy, get back here," Sandy whispered. The dog didn't listen. He just stood there and stared out the opening. "Sammy!"

The dog took a tiny step closer then doubled back to them and pushed his head into their little huddle.

More movement outside . . . then nothing.

"Come on, we need to move. Out the back," Jill said. Sandy didn't budge. "We have to." She took a look at her husband's blood on the carpet and the long smear of dirt that led back out the front. She bit back the tears, but they trickled anyway. "Now, Sandy. Now."

Slowly, they stood. Sammy still pressed himself against their legs.

Movement again . . . then an all-out trample.

The giant gator filled the front opening and eyed its

prey.

The girls shrieked. Sammy barked but was quickly silenced when the thing growled.

"Backwards," Jill said and pulled Sandy toward the back. Her daughter complied and they inched their way to the patio door.

The gator barreled toward them, quickly followed by the other, who tried to squeeze its way in between the wreckage before the first one could come through all the way. One of the gators was smaller than the other and Jill saw the parallel between human and gator, staring at each other.

The bigger one wasted no time and headed toward them. Adrenaline and fear taking over, Jill shoved Sandy at the door, even opened it for her, and pushed her outside. Sammy scurried between their legs then stood on the patio, barking.

Jill turned back, her goal to step outside and immediately close the patio door. Instead, a giant mouth came at her, its fore teeth smashing into her face and locking on. The world turned black with smears of red. Behind her, Sandy screamed and screamed.

The pain sent shockwaves down Jill's body as she was jerked forward and landed on something rough and soft.

A tongue.

Already her back felt the phantom pains of teeth crushing down into her. She tried to shove her way backward out of the thing's mouth with her palms but instead was dumped forward as the gator presumably angled its head back to swallow her. She landed in its throat. The muscles surrounding her squeezed as it tried to swallow her down. They pressed in from either side, forcing the air from her lungs.

Pressure.

Pressure.

She slipped back partway into the thing's mouth and teeth cut her arms from her body.

Sandy screamed somewhere . . . way over there . . . far away and behind.

The gator dumped her forward in its mouth again and the muscles clamped around her—and didn't let go.

* * *

Spinning in panic, arms outspread, Sandy relived the moment her mother went into the thing's mouth over and over again. Sammy barked at her heels. She looked through the patio door's glass. The big gator stayed in the living room; the smaller one came charging toward her. It smashed through the glass, sending a spray of it at her. She raised her arms to protect herself and sting after sting from the barrage of cuts against her forearms was almost a relief from the pain she felt inside.

Run.

It could've been a thought. Could've been her own voice. Could've been her mother's spirit talking to her.

Run.

Just . . . run.

Sandy tore off across the patio, hit the grass on the other side and ran into the trees. Sammy was right behind her, then past her, then back by her side. Branches snapped as the gator tore after her. Deep down, she knew there was no way she was going to outrun this thing.

Her legs felt like mush and it took all her concentration to dig her heels in and press them into the ground to propel herself forward. Thin tree branches whipped against her. She dodged around other trees. She moved right, she moved left . . . and didn't know why. Perhaps a subconscious effort to confuse and evade the monster at her heels.

Branches kept breaking behind her.

I'mdoomedI'mdoomedI'mdoomed.

Sammy was ahead of her again then gone completely. She wanted to call out his name but was too out of breath to do so. It was either keep sprinting or slow down and shout for the dumb dog.

She kept going, hoping to hit a clearing.

Branches.

Breaking.

Sammy beside her again.

A flash of dark green filled her lower peripheral and Sammy was tossed into the air and through the trees.

With a shout, Sandy looked over her shoulder; the behemoth just finished spinning around. It must have whipped its tail at the dog. She didn't know if Sammy was still alive.

The trees began to thin and she was out by the lake, the shore loaded with mostly pebbles and only a small amount of sand.

"If I go in the water, I'm dead," she breathed. Her lungs burned and she coughed up what felt like her guts. Sick from running, she turned her attention to the sound of breaking foliage. The gator emerged, then slowed, and opened its mouth as if in an attempt to show its fierceness. Giant, blood-stained teeth spiked out from an enormous mouth.

There was no hope.

The creature snapped its jaws shut and brought its head low to the ground. Sandy didn't know if this was common hunting behavior for an alligator. The Discovery Channel had never been her thing. Give her *The Bachelor* or *American Ninja Warrior* any day over that.

And even if this was genuine gator-hunting behavior—it didn't matter. These things—whatever they were— probably wouldn't act normal anyway.

The beast inched toward her.

Sandy backed up, her feet breaking the shoreline and standing in a few inches of water. She moved to bolt to the left and just as the gator moved to chase after her, Sammy appeared in front of the thing, barking his head off.

The gator stopped and eyed the dog.

"Sammy . . ." She could barely say his name.

The Golden Retriever barked and growled, seemingly willing to do anything to protect his master.

The gator focused on the dog and Sandy knew she had to take advantage of the moment to try and get away. Tears filled her eyes. *I'm so sorry, Sammy. I love you. But thank you.*

She took off down the beach and didn't look back when the dog screeched and yelped.

* * *

Wilma peeled the RCMP cruiser into town and nearly swerved into the guy in the other lane. The only guy in his car out here. Most people walked from shop to shop, place to place. Cedarhaven was a cabineer's town. Some grocery, a couple of clothing stores, an old theatre that played shows long after their release date.

Rodge's Grocery was just down the street and probably the most fortified building in the town. Steel construction. At least, it seemed so, from the outside with all its tin paneling. It was a small, converted air force hangar back when Cedarhaven wasn't even Cedarhaven but an army base during World War 2.

"Bart, find the button for the siren. Or switch, or whatever," she told him.

Bart fumbled with the switches. One turned on the radio and AC/DC blared "Highway to Hell" through the car's speakers. "Hey," he said, picking up the handheld for dispatch. He pressed the button on the side. "Ten-four, ten-four. Um . . . roger. Hello?"

"I don't think it's on," she told him.

He played with the switches and tried talking again. "Hello? Anybody there?"

Nothing.

Useless, Wilma thought. She meant the radio. Instead, she leaned her head out the driver's side opening and shouted, "Alligators! Alligators! Freakin' dinosaur alligators!"

The few people walking the sidewalks looked at her but that was about all.

Rodge's Grocery's parking lot had quite a few cars in it. She sped in and parked in front of the doors.

"Get inside," she told Bart.

The kid obeyed and opened the door and held it for her.

Wilma burst in. "Alligators!"

9

Those in the store all looked at her and Wilma felt her face flush red.

"Dinosaurs!" Bart shouted, as if thinking he was helping. It made her feel even more embarrassed. But embarrassed of what? She just told the truth.

Everyone looked on in silence. Rodger stood behind the register, both he and the customer looking her way. Rodger's eyes seemed abnormally white in contrast to his black skin.

Wilma swallowed the dry lump in her throat. "Alligators. Big ones. Killing" —she swallowed again— "people."

"Huge," Bart said, raising his hands and making himself resemble a Y.

A few of the customers muttered amongst themselves. A couple resumed eyeing the aisles for whatever it was they were shopping for.

Rodger came out from the counter with the till and drew in close. He eyed her up and down. She did the same. Blood spattered her clothes in a few places. Gently, he said, "Where's Fred?" It was what he'd called Bill for years. She'd heard every Flintstones joke in the book about her name and normally she hated it. This time she was too tired and too scared to care.

She sobbed the word "Dead" then put her face in her hands. Bart hugged her around the waist.

Rodger looked out at everyone in the store. "Everyone just mind your business. She's all right. Just shaken up. I'll be with you all in a moment." To Wilma, "Come here." He put his arm around her shoulder and drew her to the swinging half door that led behind the counter. Behind that was the store's office. He got her inside and closed the door behind them. Bart took up a spot leaning against the wall, his little face filled with concern. Rodger sat Wilma down on the office's chair and knelt before her.

"Why don't you tell me what happened?" he asked. After a pause, he added, "Is that blood?"

Wilma slowly removed her hands from her face. She didn't know where to begin.

* * *

Sandy hoofed it along the beachline until the sand gave way to a gathering of rocks. She'd have to go back into the forest if she was to make it to town.

Ugh. I was just there, she thought, *and it's not a short hike.*

The trees seemed taller all of the sudden; the bushes seemed thicker. Any dark patch or the bark of a fallen tree made her shudder.

They could be anywhere in here, she thought. *Or not in here at all.* The best she could do was step as quietly as she could and make as little noise as possible.

Her heart sped and her hands tingled. "Okay," she whispered. "You know what you saw. Godzilla. Correction: Godzillas. Big, green and nasty. Deadly. Killer animals." She pressed her lips together lest she get on a rant about how they were gigantic death machines and she was nothing but their prey. Were they tracking her? Could alligators track? Did they hunt or stalk or whatever it was other predators did? She wished she knew. All she did know, however, was that she had to keep moving and get to people. As much as she normally enjoyed her alone time, she'd give anything to be around someone, even a crowd. Safety in numbers.

She moved through the forest as quietly as possible,

each time her foot stepped on leaves or branches seemed like a bold and loud announcement of her presence.

Please don't hear me, please don't hear me. "Please don't hear me."

She stopped and took a quick moment to expel all the air from her lungs and took a deep breath. It slowed her heart some and a bit more energy filled her. "Just get to the road and follow it to town. If you see something, run like hell."

She couldn't believe she was giving herself a pep talk. Crazy people spoke to themselves and she'd be damned if she labeled herself crazy. Was she? Did she really see giant alligators? Did all that happened really happen? Was she dreaming or hallucinating or caught in some weird psycho cycle in her head where she saw all this but in real life was acting out an untrue fantasy with others looking on wondering what was wrong with her? She thought of old people with dementia and how their minds slipped and how they didn't know what year it was or would have conversations in the present with people they knew decades prior? Could that sort of thing hit at any age?

You can't be crazy. You can't. "You just can't," she said firmly.

Movement in the forest. Could be anything: a deer, a bear, even a damn little squirrel scurrying about.

Or an alligator.

A big one.

A big two.

She picked up her pace and leaves and twigs crunched beneath her feet. She immediately slowed down when her ears picked up her own noise. She stood—frozen—and listened.

All was quiet.

A bird chirped.

The wind blew a light breeze, rustling some leaves.

Her heart jumped at what was normally a pleasant and soothing sound.

Slow. Go slow. But quick, she told herself.

Sandy continued through the forest. The road couldn't

be far off.

A low growl sent her running.

* * *

To Wilma's surprise, Rodger's expression didn't change one bit as she relayed all that happened up until she burst in the doors of the grocery store. Rodger had always been a hard man to read, and even now he was sticking to character.

"I'm going to get you a cup of coffee," he said, then turned to Bart: "And a Gatorade for you."

"No gators for me, sir, nuh-uh."

"A juice box then."

"Fruit punch, if you got."

"Pretty sure I do." Rodger left the room.

Wilma was pretty sure caffeine was a bad idea and would only aggravate her nerves, but she could also use the boost. Exhaustion was setting in and she felt her eyes getting heavy. Maybe if she put her head down on Rodger's desk and fell asleep, she'd awake in her bed back at the cabin—perhaps even back at home—and this whole thing would've been some drawn-out, life-like nightmare.

"Mom?" Bart asked. "Are we trapped?"

"I don't know, honey," she said. "Come here."

He pushed off from the wall and fell into her arms. The two held each other until Rodger returned with the drinks.

As Wilma took a sip of the hot coffee, there was a knock at the office door. It was Larry, the local handyman. Mid-thirties and single, so far as anyone knew, but if you had something broken that needed fixing, he was your man no matter what it was.

"They need you up front, Rodge," Larry said. " L o t s of people wanting to pay and get out of here. Big line up."

"Okay," Rodger said. He took Wilma's hands in his. "I'll be right back."

All she could do was nod.

Rodger left again.

Bart slurped on his juice box. When he removed the straw from his mouth, he said, "The gators are coming. I just know it."

10

Sandy's legs had given up running ten minutes ago. Her heart, however, had not quit its gallop.

It's okay, it's okay. You're gonna be okay, she thought. As if she believed it. *Who am I kidding? I've gonna get eaten alive. Big teeth and some kind of massive tongue that's gonna wrap around me like a hot, slobbery blanket.*

She kept to the shoulder of the road, her eyes darting about. That thing—or things—were going to come out of the forest at any second and get her.

Don't think about that. Just get to town.

She kept on for a little longer then heard the blessed sound of tires crunching on gravel somewhere up ahead of her.

"Oh, thank God," she said.

Soon a car appeared, and she debated going into the middle of the road so it would see her clearly. *No, that's out in the open. Stay to the side.*

Her heart sped up even more. *But the car!*

The car drew nearer, but she couldn't make out the driver. She waved her arms above her head in giant crisscrosses. "Hey! Hey! Pull over!"

The car was not far now, maybe a hundred feet.

"Hey!"

The cracking of branches soon replaced the sound of crunching gravel as one of the gators barreled out of the woods and charged at the car. It slammed right into the side of the car, causing the vehicle to swerve to the side. The gator knocked the thing right off course and the car slammed into a tree on the side of the road. Even from where she stood, Sandy heard the screams coming from within. The gator rammed the car again, this time open-mouthed. Its teeth caught on the door and it jerked the door off when it backed up.

The screams turned to shrieks . . . then Sandy quickly snapped a hand to her mouth when she realized one of the shrieks belonged to herself.

The gator stuffed its mammoth snout into the opening it created, forcing its head into the car. Blood burst out at the seams where its head met the frayed framing.

Sandy's feet were suddenly moving beneath her. What was she doing? Was she crazy? She was running toward the giant gator!

Move to the side! she told herself. *Move to the side!* She went right, sprinting past where the gator gorged on the car's passengers, its bulky movement rocking the car side-to-side.

It doesn't see you, Sandy thought. At least, she hoped it didn't. Town was not far from here. She should be there soon.

"Oh please, I hope you didn't see me," she said in between breaths as she gave it all she had and headed toward Cedarhaven.

* * *

"Now, now, everybody stay calm," Rodger said as he put customers through the till. "She's just panicked, is all, saw something that wasn't there."

"I think she might be going crazy," Mrs. Berners said and placed four cans of mushroom soup on the counter.

"Now let's not be talking about her like that. Let's just carry on as normal. I'll take care of her and her boy."

"Still crazy, if you ask me," Mrs. Berner said, her face like stone.

Rodger thought it best not to start a debate so put Mrs. Berner and her soup through and let her be on her way. He did worry about Wilma, though. That poor woman. And little Bart. That poor kid seeing his mother unravel like that. What really went on out there?

Dinosaurs, he thought. *Yeah, right.* He raised his eyebrows. But giant alligators? Don't know which idea is crazier. For a second, he entertained the thought and wondered if he should shut down the store, maybe even keep everyone inside in case those things came and . . . . *No! Stop it. Don't let a panicking woman make you crazy, too.*

He kept putting through customers. More came in the store. He had hoped for a lull so he could go back and talk to Wilma, find out what really happened, but his first duty was to those who supported him and his family through buying groceries so he kept his head down and kept working.

A half-hour or so later, his ears picked up the faint sound of a girl yelling something outside. He couldn't make it out.

Rodger kept working and helped someone grab a big bag of flour and put it in their cart.

That sound outside . . . it got closer.

The voice sounded young. Sounded scared.

Sounded—He finally picked up the word, long and drawn out: "Help!"

* * *

"Alligators! Giant, big ass alligators!" Sandy shrieked as she came bursting through the doors, startling Rodger. "Everybody out! Everybody stay! Everybody" —she broke down into sobs— "I don't know."

It took Rodger a second to register the moment. He glanced at his customers. They all looked as bewildered as the others had been when Wilma had come crashing through the doors.

So it's true, then, he thought, not believing he was actually thinking it. "Giant alligators," he whispered. Out of one corner of his eye, he caught a customer glancing his way. He wasn't sure if his quiet comment had been heard.

He got out from behind the till and caught Sandy just as she crumbled to her knees.

"It . . . it ate my dog," she said through her tears.

Rodger heard a door open and Wilma and Bart came out. She looked as startled as he felt.

Quietly, Wilma approached them and got down low and put her arm around the girl.

"There, there, honey. You're safe now," Wilma said.

Rodger was surprised at Wilma's calm demeanor, considering not long before she was falling apart herself. Bart looked on, a worried expression on his young face.

The boy put his hands on his hips then looked Rodger in the eye. "See. Told you."

All Rodger could do was silently nod.

Murmuring started amongst the customers.

"What's going on?" one said.

"I don't know," another replied.

"Madness," said someone else.

"Giant alligators? Ha!" a teen said then burst out laughing.

Everybody stay in. Sandy's words from before filled Rodger's head. He didn't know what was going on but now had no choice but to give these girls plause to their claim. Even Bart.

He stood. "Everyone?" All eyes turned in his direction. "From here on out, this store's on lockdown. I can't force you to stay, but do suggest it. Something strange is going on and, it seems, it's not safe out there."

Some people nodded. Others merely hefted their baskets before the till as if signaling him to get back to his station.

One guy—Big Trev—slammed his basket on the floor. "This is stupid," he said and marched right for the exit.

When he brushed shoulders with Rodger, Rodger said, "Please reconsider."

Big Trev looked down at the girls then back up at

Rodger. "I'd rather take my chances with the"—he made quotation marks with his fingers—"'alligators.'" He headed for the door and just before leaving he said to everyone, "Don't any of you idiots remember that gators don't live in the lakes here?" He shook his head. "Stupid people." And left.

A couple others followed his lead and for a brief moment, Rodger felt like he was one of the idiots Big Trev talked about. Then he heard Wilma say to Sandy, "It's all right now. You're safe."

"I'm locking the doors," Rodger told everyone. He didn't wait to see if anyone else would go. As he turned the metal deadbolts, he hoped they were strong enough to keep out whatever was outside.

* * *

"Alligators. Pft," Big Trev said as he climbed into his truck. He put it in reverse, backed out of his spot, then left the parking lot and headed down the road. Not five minutes later, he saw a giant gator lumbering toward him.

11

Big Trev nailed the brakes on his Dodge Ram. "Holy—"

The gator faced him head-on, its body as big and wide as the truck he took so much pride in.

His head spun from the mammoth beast of dark green scales before him . . . then suddenly cleared as if it made perfect sense for him to be staring at what reminded him of Godzilla.

"Gator or some damn monster, you're dead," he said and floored it.

The Ram kicked off the gravel and soon was doing eighty, then a hundred, then one-ten, then one-fif—he plowed into the gator, its giant body mashing down on the front of the truck. Metal creaked as it bent and tore. Plastic shattered. His windshield collapsed.

Trev's nose pressed up against the gator's. Its hot breath funked up the air around him.

"Oh sh—" he started just as the gator's jaw widened and burst toward him.

* * *

All eyes fell on Wilma. Hers immediately fell on Rodger. It was like she had suddenly stolen command from a captain of his ship. Did the people believe Sandy? Did they believe *her*? Giant alligators? And even if not giant alligators specifically, did they at least believe Rodger something was seriously wrong?

It seemed so.

"What are we going to do?" Sandy asked her.

"We do what Rodger said and stay here for now. Safety in numb—"

"I don't think that applies here. The more people together, the bigger the feast. It's a buffet line in here."

Sandy was right about that. If the gators got in here, they'd tear the people and the place apart . . . but being inside with supplies was better than being outside without anything.

Wilma glanced around for Rodger. He wasn't with them anymore. She looked to Bart. "Know where Rodger went?"

"Saw him go into the office again," he said.

"Wait right here," she told him and Sandy.

Wilma went to the office and found Rodger opening up what she originally thought was a filing cabinet.

It was a gun cabinet.

For rifles . . . but it only housed one.

His back to her, Rodger pulled it out. "Double-barreled shotgun. This thing would drop a stampeding elephant if it had to."

Wilma pressed her lips together.

"We might need it," he said.

"So you do believe me. Um, us."

He turned to face her, the weapon seeming to be at the ready. "I believe that there's trouble and it doesn't hurt to be prepared. Besides" —he eyed the barrel up and down— "it might help others feel safe."

Wilma wasn't one for guns and they always set her at unease, but a weapon was better than no weapon and she doubted there was anything else in the store that could be used against the gators if needed.

She just hoped no one else was out there with those creatures roaming around.

12

Harold—Harry—squinted against the sunlight burning through the windshield as he drove the old station wagon down the gravel road. His wife, Harriette, sat beside him, knitting. What she was making, he didn't know. They all started out as scarves until they became something else and that's what it looked like to him right now.

The two "Harrys."

He hated when people called them that, but who was he to pick the name of the woman he fell in love with forty-nine years ago?

"Keep your eyes on the road," Harriette said. "I see you peeking."

He swore the woman had eyes all over her head, looking every which way, and not just in the back.

"Sorry," he said.

There wasn't much to see on the ride into town. Tonight was steak night and Rodge's Grocery was just the place to get it. Thick cuts; something unheard of in small lake towns. And deer steak, no less. That was a treat out here. Beef in the city; deer lakeside.

Harry noticed his wife peering out the window. Normally, he didn't care what she looked at, but something about the way her eyes squinted and how she slightly turned in her chair made him curious. "What?"

"Hm? Oh, nothing. Just thought I saw something

strange."

"Oh yeah? Like what?"

"A moving tree."

"A moving tree," he said. "Okay, then."

"Not walking upright. Horizontal. Huge. Like the thing had broken over but instead of staying put was making its way through the forest like a slow train."

"Whatever you say, my love."

"Is that sarcasm I detect?"

"Who, me? No. Of course not." He winked.

"Just keep your eyes on the road. I'm hungry."

* * *

Wilma didn't know what to make of any of it. Well, she did. She understood what was happening—mentally—but her heart, the part of her with true acceptance, still had a hard time believing there were two giant alligators out there with human beings on their mind as prey. She supposed Sandy felt the same way or, at least, something similar.

She looked to her son. Poor Bart. He'd lost his father and his brother to monsters that could not be explained. Monsters that didn't seem to function like their smaller counterparts. She wondered if, though on the outside the two beasts appeared like alligators, they were indeed what they presented themselves to be. Perhaps they were some prehistoric creatures that had somehow thawed from somewhere else—somehow still alive—and had made their way here? Or, perhaps, they were a couple of genetic experiments gone wrong? Or, even, they were as yet an undiscovered species on the planet and were only making their debut now.

She didn't know and, for right now, she didn't want to know. All she knew was that they were dangerous and were among the strongest beasts on the planet, if not *the* strongest. If there were more of them out there, it'd only be a matter of time before humanity fell at their scaly feet.

Only a matter of time before human beings no longer

ruled the Earth.

In the background, Rodger was on the phone calling the neighboring businesses to lock down their doors as well.

She put an arm around Bart's shoulder and squeezed him in tight. Wilma knew there might not be anything she could do to save him, but what she could do was provide him warmth and love in what could be his last day—even last hours—on Earth.

Bart leaned into her. She felt his body shake with a sniffle.

"Are we going to be all right, Mom?" he asked.

I don't know. "Yes, sweetie. Of course. Everything will be all right." She wished she could believe it herself.

* * *

"Shouldn't take long to get what we need," Harry said as he drove into Rodge's Grocery's parking lot.

"You and your 'in-and-out,'" Harriette said. "I'm going to browse. You do what you want."

"Whatever you say, boss." Once Harry pulled into his stall, he noticed the parking lot was dead quiet. Nine times out of ten there was at least one person coming out of the store when he pulled up, with at least one other person going in. Today, there was nobody. He checked left, then he checked right. The street was quiet as well, not a soul in sight.

Strange, he thought, then dismissed the notion of something being wrong. Cedarhaven was just what its name claimed to be: a haven away from the rat race of the city and the hustle and bustle of life. Even stress. Out here—out here was its own world: calm and peaceful. There was a lightness of soul that took place the moment you drove into town. All your worries, all your cares vanished, and all that mattered was time with loved ones and a relaxing getaway.

Harry and his wife exited their vehicle and made their way toward the store's doors.

13

Wilma saw Harry and his wife make their way to the store's doors. She shifted her gaze to Rodger, who eyed the couple carefully. Then his eyebrows raised in almost indecisiveness.

He can't possibly be considering not letting them in, is he? she thought.

Harry stepped up to the door and tried to open it. It didn't budge. He looked the door up and down then tried again. Same thing.

Locked.

He put his hand to his forehead like a makeshift peak and peered in. The puzzlement on his face said he saw everyone else in there. He jiggled on the door handle. "Hey, Rodge. You closed or something? Open? Whatchya all doing in there?"

Rodger moved from his post and stepped toward the door. His gaze moved from Harry to Harriette, to past them, then back to them. He started to move quickly.

"Hey, open up. Me and the Mrs. have got some shopping to do," Harry said through the glass.

Rodger gave them a wave and, Wilma supposed, would fill them in on what was going on once the elderly couple was inside.

Rodger reached for the various locks, twisted them, then suddenly twisted them back.

What the hell? Wilma thought.

Sandy started whimpering.

"Let us in!" Harry said, the man's brows scrunched.

Harriette had a hand on her husband's arm in a presumed effort to calm him down.

Rodger slowly shook his head.

"Whaddya mean no?" Harry said.

"Rodger, what's wrong?" Harriette asked.

Rodger slowly stepped away from the door, and it was then Wilma saw the behemoth make its way out of the woods across the road.

"What're you stepping away for?" Harriette asked.

"Yeah," Harry said.

Rodger slowly raised a finger and pointed behind them.

Harry squinted. "What?"

"Behind you!"

"Huh?"

"Turn around!" Wilma screamed, running up beside Rodger.

"Mom!" Bart said.

Harry and Harriette turned around to see the giant alligator stepping toward them. Harriette fainted. Harry spun around and banged on the glass then started ramming into it with his shoulder. He finally noticed his wife, passed out on the ground. He tugged on her shoulders in violent jerks, trying to get her to her feet.

The alligator kept coming.

The old man kicked at the door. "Rodger!"

"I can't, Harry, I'm sorry," Rodger said, then, to everyone else: "Hide! Hide, dammit!"

Wilma jerked Bart by the arm and dragged him down to the end of one of the aisles, his little legs barely keeping up. "Ow, you're hurting me," he said. They got behind the aisle and had a clear view to the front doors.

Rodger stood there, frozen, most likely not sure if he should let them in and make a ruckus or hide with everyone else. By saving the two elderly people outside, he could jeopardize them all. Slowly, he backed away from the door.

"No! Rodger! No!" Harry shouted. The old man turned and pulled on his wife again. He managed to get his hands under her armpits and dragged her part way into the parking lot, probably for their vehicle.

The alligator stared them down then slowly opened its giant jaws.

Wilma put her hand over Bart's eyes. He put his hands on hers and pressed her hand against his eyes even harder.

Outside, the gator slowed its movement as Harry scrambled to get Harriette to their vehicle. It didn't attack, but inched forward, mouth open. Quickly, from behind, the other gator came and clamped its mouth around Harry, tossed him up in the air, then opened wide and let Harry fall into its mouth in one gulp. Before the echo of Harry's scream could end, the second gator moved in and bit into Harriette's limp body, a spray of blood indicating she was instantly dead.

Rodger started sobbing. Wilma's heart ached. The guilt the man must feel. She slowly stood to go to his side, but he saw her and waved her to hide.

"They . . . they can't see us," he said, his voice barely audible. "Stay down."

* * *

Bart peeled his mom's hand from his face. "Did he . . . was he . . . . Eww, gross."

Wilma followed his line of sight to the smear of blood on the pavement. "Bart, don't look at that." But it was already too late. The kid seemed mesmerized by the gore. He slowly stood and started walking toward the front entrance.

"Get down," someone said in a loud whisper.

"Bart!" Wilma said, her voice the same volume.

"C'mere, son," Rodger said and yanked the kid aside.

At least he'll be safe with him, Wilma thought or, at least, hoped.

All eyes in the grocery store were fixated on the gators on the other side of the glass doors. The two monsters stared at each other. One was bigger than the other by about fifty percent. Wilma supposed it could be a younger gator and its mother. Maybe even the father. Their identities were a moot point anyway. They were out there. She and her fellow havenites were in here. If nobody moved or made any noise, they wouldn't draw attention to themselves.

She thought back to Bart's adamancy the creatures outside were dinosaurs. She thought of a T-Rex and wondered if, like their prehistoric ancestor, their vision was based on movement. She doubted it.

The gators stood stone still.

"Rodge," someone whispered. "Is there a back door to this place?"

"Of course," he whispered back loud and clear.

"Then let's all slowly make our way back there and get the hell out of here."

Wilma thought it was a great idea and wanted to move but didn't want to do it without her son.

"No noise," Rodger said. "Carefully. Slowly. Hold your breath if you have to."

There was some murmuring amongst the crowd about the idea, their voices—though quiet—seemed suddenly loud compared to all the silence before.

Wilma checked on the gators. The smaller one slowly swayed its head side to side while the other remained perfectly still.

With a loud crash, the smaller gator swung its tail into a car. The larger gator moved past it and did the same.

Were they playing a game? Surely not.

Again they swatted their tails into a couple cars.

A few screams erupted inside the store. That's when both gators turned their attention on the doors and started coming toward them.

14

Sandy went into hysterics and all Wilma wanted to do was rush over to the girl and clamp her mouth shut. Already folks were running for the back door; one guy trampled Rodger to the ground. The moment Wilma took her eyes off the store owner and back to the doors, she saw Sandy standing near the front door mats, hopping and screaming.

"I don't want to die," she said. "I don't want to die!"

Rodger got up off the floor and pointed the shotgun at the gators. The two giant reptiles took out the glass doors like they were nothing, sending forth a shimmering shower of what could be mistaken as ice. Sandy's palms went to her eyes and Wilma could only assume she got glass in them. Sandy rubbed at her eyes and soon red bloody circles masked her blue eyes in blood.

Bart shrieked as Rodger let loose with the shotgun, pumping round after round into the biggest of the two gators while it opened its mouth and bit Sandy in half. The girl's legs went flying into separate aisles while the creature chewed on her torso. The smaller gator plowed into the aisles, knocking them over, sending food and wares flying.

The relentless boom of the shotgun made Wilma's ears ring.

Bart kept screaming and she cursed herself for not making a break for it instead of simply watching the grizzly sight before her. She picked up Bart and carried the wailing kid toward the back. She glanced over her shoulder to see Rodger get squished by one of the gator's enormous feet, its clawed toes busting bloody holes into Rodger's head and chest.

For a split second, she debated trying to steal the shotgun for herself, but when the smaller gator rushed to the bigger gator's side and chowed down on what was left of Rodger, she continued her dash for the back door. When she got there, most of the people had funneled out.

"I got a kid," she yelled. "Let me through. Please. I beg you."

No one paid her any mind.

The gators were right behind them.

Wilma forced her way into the crowd and her heart broke the moment the gators' growls turned to wet crunches of bone as the people she passed became dinner.

She burst outside, looked left then right, then remembered the RCMP car. She'd have to round the building to get to it and she couldn't recall if her vehicle had been one of the ones the gators had smashed. She didn't know if she should risk it.

Dammit, go for it, she thought. *You have to. Only way to outrun them.*

Screams poured out from the backdoor. One guy she recognized as Larry dove out the door only to be dragged back in by a large mouth filled with sharp teeth.

"MommyMommyMommy," Bart said.

"It's okay, baby. I got you." She ran with him around to the front of the store to the parking lot out front. Nearly all the vehicles were totalled, including the RCMP vehicle. Heart racing, legs surging with energy from adrenaline, she ran down the street. "Help! Help!"

Behind her, wood cracked as the two gators stormed through what was left of the front of the store. The load-bearing wall both in front and partly on each side crumbled and the whole store tilted forward then crashed down in a tidal wave of debris.

The gators tore after her.

The street was empty.

Her feet slapped against the pavement as she gave it all she had then, in a crushing moment, Bart suddenly went from weighing fifty pounds to a thousand and she collapsed under his weight. He hit the pavement beside her and let out a loud "Ow." Wilma wanted to apologize then words escaped her when she saw the big red scrape across his face and her poor baby bled.

Gators behind.

Getting close.

It took all her strength to get to her feet, the adrenaline rush having totally exhausted her muscles. She could only assume Bart felt the same way. She yanked him up by the hands and pulled him in between two stores, the alley in between about three feet wide. They got about halfway through then stopped to catch their breath.

"Did they . . . did they . . . see us?" Bart asked.

Wilma swallowed the dry lump in her throat. "I don't know." *I hope not. Please, God, I hope not.*

15

"Come on, hurry," Wilma said, pulling Bart by the hand.

Bart picked up his pace, so much so that he started pulling her along.

Those gators were somewhere behind them and Wilma would be damned if she would let them get to Bart.

The two ran down the gravel road, each every so often checking over their shoulders to see if the gators followed. So far, everything seemed fine.

Bart seemed to be slowing down, too. "Mom, I need to . . . stop," he said.

"You mean your mama can run longer than you can?" However, her lungs began to burn as the exertion finally got to her and the adrenaline wore off.

He scrunched his face and made a burst for it further down the road. Wilma could scarcely breathe by the time Bart slowed down again but there was no way she'd let the little guy win.

Finally, they began walking, huffing and puffing, and still stealing glances backward.

Bart ripped his hand out of hers, turned to the side, and upchucked. For some reason, she did the same. The sound. The sight. Blech.

Overhead the sky got darker.

Wilma's stomach immediately settled when she spotted an SUV once they crested a small hill. "Bart, look!"

"Awesome."

As they got closer, Wilma couldn't see if anyone was in there through the rear window. Closer yet, and the SUV was empty.

When they approached, Bart said, "Oh man . . ."

The driver's side door to the vehicle had been torn off and the seat was darker than the others.

Blood.

Wilma peered in. The rear driver's side window was smashed and spattered across both windows on the passenger's side were gooey bits of flesh or brain. She couldn't tell which.

She checked out the driver's seat again. Then the dash. The keys were still in the ignition.

Oh, how she didn't want to sit on that seat, but there was no choice. This vehicle could be their ticket to freedom. She reached around the wheel and turned the key. The SUV came to life.

She took a deep breath then exhaled slowly. "Get in, Bart."

"No way. That's disgusting."

"The other seats aren't bad. I get to sit in the yucky one." She looked down the road. Something inside told her they should get going.

"No," he said.

"Now!"

He shook his head then walked around the vehicle and got in the front passenger seat. When Wilma settled into her own, she felt what hadn't dried of the blood dampen her pants.

They headed down the road.

* * *

They had driven for a while, Bart now fascinated with the gore on the interior of the vehicle instead of repulsed like before.

"That's definitely got to be brains," he said with confidence.

"Bart, just look forward, okay?" Wilma said.

He turned and looked at the road then back at the "brains" again.

"Bart!"

"Sorry," he said, turning around. "Sheesh."

About five minutes later, Wilma came to a fork in the road. Either route would take them away from Cedarhaven, but as to where she wanted to go, she wasn't sure.

"We'll go . . . right," she said.

Bart opened up his window and hung his head out, looking back. "I think I see something," he said.

She yanked on his shirt and pulled him back onto his seat. "Sit. Down. You don't even have your seatbelt on."

"Mom, I'm not kidding. There's something back there."

Wilma checked her rearview mirror but it was getting too dark to see anything clearly. She glanced over her shoulder. Shadows moved across the road and she wasn't sure if it was her imagination or if something was really out there. She put her eyes back on the road only to catch Bart in her peripheral half hanging out of the SUV again.

She turned more squarely toward him and jerked on his shirt. "Bart!"

Bart pointed out the window.

Wilma looked back. Shadows.

Imagined? Maybe.

Eyes back on the road.

A sharp turn appeared.

Bart out the window.

Eyes off the road.

A yank on his shirt.

The road ran out as she missed the turn. She veered to the left to take it but skidded along the gravel and soon found the SUV ka-thunking its way down a foresty hill. Within seconds a giant oak appeared in the headlights and she nailed it head-on.

Wilma jerked forward then back from the impact. Bart

slammed up against the dash as both airbags burst from their compartments.

Ringing filled Wilma's ears then all went blurry, then black and quiet for a moment. When she came around, Bart stood beside her on her side of the vehicle.

Worry covered his face. "You okay, Mom?" he asked.

Her head pounded and her neck was sore, but she seemed all right. "Yeah." She felt her face for any blood. Her skin was damp but in the dim light of the headlights, it revealed it was sweat, not blood.

"Are you okay?" she asked.

"My shoulders and neck hurt, but I didn't break anything."

Through the dizziness that swept over her, all she could do was nod. Wilma stumbled out of the vehicle and landed on her knees, her lower back suddenly locking up.

"What do we do now, Mom?" Bart asked.

She tried straightening and it hurt like the dickens. "I'm not sure, but I'll think of something."

* * *

It was almost fully dark now and Wilma and Bart stood by the side of the road hoping somebody would drive by.

Surely the gators hadn't gotten everyone? Wilma thought.

"I'm cold," Bart said. Without the day's hot sun and the north wind blowing through, Wilma felt the chill, too.

She put her arm around his shoulder and gave it a rub. "It'll be all right. Somebody will turn up."

Minutes passed.

Nothing.

More minutes.

No one was coming.

A rustle in the bushes across the way.

Bart pressed in closer to his mother.

She'd heard it, too, and hoped to goodness it was just a deer or a rabbit making its way through the woods.

The sound stopped and the two waited. Bart began to

hop in little jumps. "I'm coooold."

More rustling and the crack of a few branches . . . then a big black shape emerged and stepped out onto the road.

Bart screamed. The thing grew in size as it stood on its hind legs. Wilma shrieked. The bear growled back.

All strength ran from her legs as she turned to run the hell away, and she stumbled with her hand still around Bart's shoulder. He tripped with her and the next thing she knew both of them were running and losing their footing, then the world went head over heels and heels over head and Wilma rolled down the tree-filled hill, bouncing back and forth between tree trunks like in a pinball until she finally rolled to a stop. Her world swam; her stomach sloshed in waves. She tried getting up but couldn't steady herself enough so leaned against a tree.

"Bar" —she spat the leaves and dirt from her mouth— "Bart? Bart!" *Oh crap, don't yell. The bear. The—* "Bart!"

"Over . . . here . . ." came his small voice.

She followed its direction. It was so dark she couldn't see much of anything except the black ground and gray of the trees. Most of the light was hidden by the canopy overhead.

"Mom . . ." he said.

She finally found him and took hold of him. She felt his face and neck for any obvious injuries.

"Did you see that thing?" he asked.

"Oh yeah."

"Pretty cool, huh?"

She swatted his shoulder. "No."

More movement somewhere in the trees. The ground wasn't steep here so they were at the bottom of the hill.

"Come on," she said.

"We can't go up the hill. The bear will eat us."

Wilma listened carefully. Somewhere ahead of them was the lapping of water. Despite all that driving, they still hadn't gone past the lake.

She led him in that direction but solely so they could get their bearings. Then it'd be back up the hill somewhere further down to follow the road.

Her back and shoulders tensed as she led her son through the dark of the forest. Anything could be out here.

Anything.

16

Bart looked up overhead. The dark canopy of tree leaves blanketed all that was around them in a light charcoal. Walking was slow and more than once he reached out ahead of him to feel for any upcoming trees or bushes.

"Mom?" Bart asked.

"Yes?"

"Dinosaurs were as big as trees, right?"

"Most of them, I think," she replied. "Why?"

"These alligators can't be dinosaurs, then. They're not as tall as the trees."

"I don't know what they are, sweetie," Wilma said. "All I know is we need to get as far away from here as possible."

"I don't like being in the dark," Bart said.

"Me neither."

"Why can't we go back to the road?"

Wilma stopped walking. So did he. "We're a little turned around and I'm not sure which way the road is. I don't want to lead us deeper into the woods."

Wind blew through the canopy above, giving Bart a startle. "But it's halfers. We go one way and we could be on the road. Go the other way and we're into lots of trees. Half and half."

She drew him in close. Despite the chilly night, he still felt her warmth. "I don't want to lead us the wrong way and 'halfers' leaves too much chance for a mistake."

Bart's heart sank at his idea being shot down, but he understood her reasoning. Kinda. He saw it more like flipping a coin, but, he guessed, his mother saw it as something else.

A tree branch snapped behind them, then what sounded like something rough scraping against tree bark followed.

"Come on," Wilma whispered, taking him by the hand.

The sound grew louder.

"We're being followed," Bart said.

His mom didn't reply.

Can't be one of those gators, he thought. *The trees are too close together.* The notion brought him some comfort, but after remembering that bear on the road, all reassurance left him.

More branches snapping, more scraping. Footfalls. Slow.

"We're being hunted," Bart whispered.

"Don't say that," Wilma replied.

"It's the truth."

"Don't say that." Her tone was firm.

The footfalls ceased. And they weren't really footfalls, but Bart wasn't sure what else to call them. Pawfalls?

The footfalls increased and something crashed into the back of Bart's legs, sending him sprawling forward and scraping his chin across the ground.

"Bart!" his mom said. She crouched down beside him. "Are you all—" She stopped when the growl sounded.

* * *

The wolf eyed the two of them, and fear wrapped its cold arms around Wilma's body. Her boy still lay on the ground.

"Don't. Move," she said.

He got himself up onto his elbows. "Why? What was that—" He must have seen the wolf, too, because he suddenly stopped talking.

I don't know what to do, Wilma thought. *If we try and run away, it'll catch us in no time and who knows how many other wolves might be around us. If we stay, this stare-down is only going to last so long before the thing makes a move.*

She wished she had a horn or something to scare the thing away or get it to back off.

A loud crack sounded behind them and the wolf perked up its ears then began sniffing the air.

Branches crashed.

The wolf growled and made a dash straight for Wilma. "Bart, keep your head down!"

She didn't know if he obeyed, but the weight of the heavy wolf knocked her over and sent her on her back. It snapped its jaws and took a stinging bite out of her cheek. Wilma put up her forearms in front of her face to shield it from any more damage but the wolf bit into her arm and violently jerked its head left then right, over and over, as if trying to tear the obstruction away.

The wolf's hot breath blew so heavy its heat gave Wilma's chilled skin goosebumps.

More trees cracked and the stench of something else filled the air.

The wolf jumped back, her forearm still in its mouth, and bone cracked around her elbow. A spray of blood coated her face and its coppery taste touched her tongue.

"Bart—" she started.

Wilma looked side to side. More wolves appeared from the shadows. There had to be at least five, but the blood in her eyes made it difficult to know for sure.

"Mom!" Bart howled.

"My" —the wolf let go of her forearm and bit into her leg, sending a shockwave of pain through her thigh— "son . . ."

A guttural hiss sounded as did a low growl. The wolves stopped moving.

The trees cracked and snapped and shattered as one of the giganti-gators came in, biting at the wolves and swishing its tail so hard it took down other trees as well.

Though relieved, Wilma knew it'd only be seconds before—

The gator's jaws slammed down around either side of her like a triangular tent. They closed, scraping up her, the wolf on her legs, the dirt around her. Wilma tried to move in and sit up on the thing's tongue, but just as she started to right herself, she heard the faint sound of Bart's voice somewhere on the other side of the gator's jaws. She didn't know what he said, but she knew what she was going to say: "I love you."

The gator's tongue rocked beneath her and slammed her against the roof of its mouth just as it tilted its head back to gulp her and the wolf down. She slid partway down its throat then was jerked up close to its teeth. The gator chewed and sharp teeth pierced her ribcage, cracking it wide open. When the gator opened its mouth, she felt her lungs ripped from her body.

The teeth came down again.

Warm blood covered her.

17

Bart flew through the air and skidded across the ground after the gator's tail swatted him away. He rolled into a tree and hit his head. Groaning, he lay on his side and watched as the gator had at 'er with the wolves.

That's just one of them, he thought. *Where's the sec—*

Trees cracked and snapped and something huge barreled through the woods.

Time stood still and Bart deliberated staying where he was and hoped nothing saw him, or get to his feet and make a break for it through the woods and going halfers.

His mom . . . . His sweet mom. His dad. His brother. All taken from him.

The tears overtook him and he wracked with sobs and screams.

Time resumed and he was on his feet though didn't recall how he got to them. He tore off through the woods, getting as far away from the bloody chaos as possible.

Halfers.

He tried to recall the path his mother and him recently took after the car crashed. He hadn't paid attention the whole time she led him but he assumed they had gone in a more or less straight line. Then again, he could be totally turned around now thanks to getting tossed into the thick of the trees.

Bart went left.

His half.
Alone.

* * *

Bart cautiously made his way through the woods, a few times stubbing his toes against tree roots. Those gators were somewhere behind him because he could hear them move through the forest, hear those growls, hear the occasional animalistic yelp or cry as another creature became their dinner.

Bart whacked his shoulder against a tree, sending a vibration of pain through his arm. He collapsed to his knees and the tears flooded out. Everybody was dead. Everyone. His mom. His dad. His brother. The tears pulled from deep in his gut, went up through his aching heart, up his dry throat, and came out through wild and loud sobs, the tears running fast from his eyes.

Why, why, why, why, why, he thought, then whispered the same. The salty taste of his tears stung his tongue and made it worse.

For a moment, he dreamed of someone coming to his rescue. Some big burly lumberjack type armed to the teeth with weapons the two of them could use against the alligators. Instead, as he listened for boots stepping through the forest, he heard movement somewhere behind him and breaking trees.

Knees sore from kneeling, Bart used the tree trunk like a pole to pull himself up. He kept on.

Kept on going halfers.

There had to be something soon.

* * *

Bart awoke with a start. He sat against a tree, knees pulled up to his chest, arms crossed on top, head on his arms.

"I'm alive," he said, "or a ghost." He looked around for his dead body, and when he didn't see it, he touched the tree behind him. The wood was hard, the bark rough. If he was a ghost, his hand would've passed right through. "Not a ghost." Which was oddly a disappointment because being a ghost meant you could fly and pass through solid objects and have the power of invisibility.

The sound of water soothed Bart's ears.

"The lake!" he said. He sprang to his feet. His stomach growled from hunger. The first thing he'd do once he got to the lake was drink as much as he could despite the water being a bit dirty. From there, he might see other cabins and could get help.

He moved through the forest as quickly as he could. Twenty minutes or so later, he came out into a clearing. It wasn't a beach-beach, but a mixture of sand and grass and rocks. Didn't matter. Water. He carefully stepped across the rocks, then got momentarily distracted as images of his family crept into his mind's eye. He shoved the images away and tried to stay strong. He had to. For them. Someone needed to honor their memory. Someone needed to survive.

He crouched down on a rock close to the water, scooped his hands in, and brought the water to his lips. It tasted kind of fishy and sandy, but it didn't matter. It was water and he drank as much as he could until his stomach told him to stop or he'd yack it all up.

Bart looked up and down the shoreline. From where he stood, he couldn't see any cabins. Heart sunk, he made his way along the shore, figuring something—anything—had to show up at some point.

* * *

It must have been an hour later when Bart ascended a steep, grassy hill. He figured if the lake was behind him, the road probably ran parallel to it, so all he had to do was walk in a straight line and he'd eventually get there.

The sound of water lapping the shore behind him and the fatigue from all that had happened made him sleepy.

"No," he said. "Have to keep on going."

The hill was so steep he needed to use his hands to ascend it. He was about halfway up when his foot slipped, causing him to fall flat on his stomach. He carefully got back on all fours and climbed, but when his foot slipped again, he tumbled down the hill—sky, grass, sky, grass—until he met the sudden cold of the water.

The tears came again.

As did the blurry dark green form of what he hoped was a giant rock sticking out of the water but knew full well that wasn't the case.

Bart scrambled for shore, wildly swimming toward safety.

Something hard and sharp caught him by the feet and spun him around so he faced the expanse of the lake. He looked over his shoulder to see the giant snout and enormous eyes of the gator. The thing pulled him under the water. Bart flailed his arms and screamed as the pressure on his legs grew more and more intense.

Something had his arms.

For a second, he resurfaced then went back under again, this time inhaling a lungful of lake water.

Back above the surface, a giant gator in front and one in the back. The one behind him twisted him over, forcing his arms to turn above him, pulling his shoulder from its socket.

Screaming, Bart's insides lit on fire and through teary vision, he watched as his middle stretched and stretched until it tore completely in half.

Blood covered the water.

His blood.

Tears.

Dark.

EPILOGUE

He watched the two gators wrap their jaws on each of their half of the meal as he finally arrived after making the long journey.

The two giganti-gators swam toward him. The three looked at each other and stayed like that for a long while.

Father, mother, and son.

The alpha male turned and swam out further into the lake, the other two behind him.

It was time for more meat. An endless surplus.

Soon, they would all taste blood.

Giganti-gator Death Machine III

The three of them swam through the Pacific Ocean at ever-gathering speeds, hungry for a fresh meal. Ahead, the clear water revealed four sharks. The largest of the gators, a male, held back as the female and their sole offspring swam toward the giant fish. In an instant, the female struck one head-on, sinking her teeth into it, blood spurting through the water in crimson clouds, and tore it apart from the middle. In a flurry of motion, the female spun in the water and devoured the ocean's main predator. The smaller gator took its chances and met another shark head-on. All the young one had to do was open its giant mouth and the shark swam right into it. The gator clamped its mouth shut.

The massive male decided it was time to join the fight and propelled itself toward the nearest shark. It opened its mouth and took it in one bite. The final shark didn't retreat but instead swam straight toward the female and tried to take a bite out of its thick hide. The female swirled around and ripped the tail off the great fish before swirling again and swallowing the thing's head and the remainder of its body.

Then, as if nothing happened, the three swam on.

There was more food to be had.

PROLOGUE

Jerry Johnson had hit the jackpot. A cool thirteen million on the lotto. At times he thought it was a fluke. At others, he chalked it up to strategy: play the same numbers over and over again, none of this Quick Pick stuff. He had a conspiracy theory about the Quick Picks. He thought all those quick combinations when people bought tickets were fed into a mainframe which told the final draw *not* to pick those numbers. Whatever the case, it didn't matter. He quit his job as a grocery clerk; his wife, Darlene, quit the coffee shop and they got the heck out of Dodge, got the paperwork done, and settled in Los Angeles. It was also there he bought a yacht and named it the *Dominator* due to its size. It was one big bastard of a boat, about seventy feet long and twenty feet wide. It floated high above the water and now, out here on the ocean, Jerry felt like the king of the world. Heck, the king of *all* worlds. And it wasn't just the boat that made him feel like a king. He was young— thirty-eight—had a knockout for a wife with perfect strawberry-blonde hair and a body that even after eight years of marriage still revved his engine. Their son, Luke, a boy of eight, didn't seem to understand what happened to his family and how fortunate they'd become.

Fortunate.

Fortune.

Thirteen million dollars.

Thirteen. Million. Dollars.

Lucky number thirteen.

Jerry gazed at his wife. She lay on a long lawn chair, taking in the sun while Luke played with his Hot Wheels on the lower deck.

Not completely at home driving a yacht, Jerry decided to take it easy and just move along the coastline, taking in the beach, the surfers, those in dingies and a few others in yachts but not ones nearly as big as his. He smugly smiled as waves crashed against the boat.

"Dad, stop it!" Luke shouted from the main deck. "You just busted up my track."

"Sorry, son," he said. "Mother Nature doesn't understand the importance of Hot Wheels." He flashed his son a smile. Luke grimaced and got to work rebuilding his race-car masterpiece.

Another wave was coming up. The yacht hit it full force.

"Dad!"

"Sorry, kiddo."

Another wave and another right after.

Ahead, the water turned dark amidst its crystal clear surroundings. Jerry wasn't sure what it was. Maybe a giant rock beneath the surface, one so huge it nearly cleared the surface. Jerry tried to move around it but couldn't quite make the turn. A loud ka-thunk rocked the boat.

"Dammit, Dad!" Luke said as he sat there amongst a pile of Hot Wheel cars and tracks.

"Hey, watch your mouth!" his wife said.

"Dad keeps ruining my track."

"It's not his fault. It's the waves."

"I don't care." Then, to his father: "Do you have to hit every single—"

A massive blur of green-gray burst from the ocean's surface and came crashing down on the middle of the yacht. It cut clean through, with Jerry on one side and his wife and kid on the other. The green-gray blur burst forth again, this time swiping in sideways and decimating what was left of the boat.

Just as Jerry tumbled into the water, he saw his wife and kid do the same on the other side of the wreckage.

"What the hell—" Jerry said. Then he shouted amid the sound of the waves, "Darlene, I'm coming. Get Luke." He thought he saw her nod her acknowledgement. A wave crashed down on him and he went under. He quickly swam back to the surface and headed in the direction of his family. When he finally reached them, he was out of breath. Luke's lips quivered and Jerry knew it was from fear and not the temperature of the water. Darlene's big green eyes stared at him in askance.

"Jerry?" she said.

Jerry glanced back at the yacht. "I don't know. I don't—"

"Jer—" His wife's words were cut short and when Jerry looked back beside Luke, the water had turned red.

"Shark!" Luke cried.

Jerry immediately grabbed hold of him. "We're going to swim to shore, okay?"

Luke didn't respond but started heading toward shore. Jerry swam, simultaneously giving his son a push forward when he could. When he went to do it again, his hand just missed Luke as his son went under the water.

"Luke!" He dove beneath the surface and opened his eyes. The stinging salt water forced him to immediately close them. He grasped around, hoping to get hold of his son.

Nothing. Just water.

Just—something hard and rough like tree bark.

Jerry kicked his way to the surface.

The moment he broke through, he cried, "Darlene! Luke!"

Shark, he thought. But what did he feel under the water?

Before he could give it much thought, a giant reptilian face rose above the surface, its teeth pink with streaks of red.

Heart beating so hard and so fast, Jerry screamed then turned to swim away only to be greeted by another giant reptile head. Or was it the same one?

He thought of his wife and kid.

He thought of the yacht.

The giant head opened its enormous mouth and shoved forward into him, encasing him completely. As the teeth ripped him apart, Jerry cried from the pain.

Cried for his family.

Heck, even cried for his boat.

Lucky number thirteen.

"Can't believe this downpour," George said gazing out the window of Don't be Board. He scratched his salt-and-pepper hair and, as always, was dismayed to find it thinning out.

"Me neither," his wife Ethel said.

They sat in the games cafe with their friends of ten years, Maxwell and Lois.

"Who'd woulda thought Los Angeles could produce such weather," Maxwell said.

"Maybe we're getting all our rain at once this year then that'll be it," Lois said.

"Let's hope so," George said then focused his attention back on *King of Tokyo*.

The four of them gathered every Friday night here at Don't be Board. With all of their work schedules, it was the only night to do so.

George was a doctor and Ethel was a nurse, so their shifts varied. Maxwell was a big-shot lawyer who worked long hours, and Lois was a stay-at-home mom, which carried a crazy schedule in itself, especially in the evenings when she acted as the family chauffeur.

It was George's turn so he rolled the dice. Two attacks, two energy, two numbers. Though he could have had three rolls of the die, he left them as they were and since he was the present King of Tokyo, he let everybody have it with those two attacks.

"How's things at the hospital?" Lois asked George.

"Busy. A lot of surgeries these days. Don't know why. I've seen so much blood and guts over the past while each time I cut a patient open it's like looking at a bowl of spaghetti." He was never one to shy from the truth and always shot point-blank when asked about what he did for a living. It scared and bothered some people; others didn't mind. "Fortunately, Ethel and I have been working similar shifts so we've been taking one car in to work instead of our usual two."

Ethel simply nodded, rolled her turn, and attacked her husband on the board.

"Nice one, dear," George said.

Maxwell took a sip of his coffee, something George always found amusing. Maxwell. Maxwell House. He chuckled. It was a lame joke but it got him every time.

"You look tired," Ethel said to Lois.

Lois pulled her brown hair back in a faux ponytail then let it fall loose again. "You'd think I'd have a breather during the day while the kids are at school, but they're teenagers and the messes keep piling up. I'm tempted to just leave our house a disaster zone and claim I can't keep up with the demand."

"Don't your kids clean up after themselves?"

"Yep, which is why it's so trying. It's like they make a mess, clean it, then go back at it with a vengeance as if they're mad at the organizing they did."

The floor vibrated, which caught George off guard. He lifted his feet then set them back down. He figured a bunch of people must have pulled their chairs out at one time thus causing the tremor.

The game went on for another twenty minutes and George emerged victorious as the King of Tokyo.

"Anyone up for round two?" he asked. "Twenty bucks says I'll beat you."

Lois checked her watch. George did the same. It was 9:46 pm.

"I'd like to," Lois said, "but the kids are at home and it's getting late."

"Come on, they can take care of themselves," Maxwell said.

Lois shot him a hot glare.

"I mean, you're right. It is getting late. Time to boogie."

Lois stood from the table and pulled on her coat. George could see it wasn't designed for rain. "Now I get to be soaked to the bone."

"Don't worry," Maxwell said, "when we get home, I'll warm ya."

She gave him a playful smile. George merely smirked. Ethel seemed too busy packing up to notice.

"Thanks for the wonderful evening," Lois said.

Ethel rose from her chair and Lois hugged her while the two men shook hands.

"Ready?" Maxwell asked his wife.

"Yep." Then, "You should've worn a coat."

"But it was so nice when we got here."

"That's what you get for not planning ahead."

"How was I supposed to know God would dump a bucket on us."

"I think it's His weather machine guy who's to blame."

"Isn't He the weather machine guy?"

She didn't answer him. To Maxwell and Lois: "Thanks again. Same time next week?"

George and Ethel quickly exchanged glances. "Yep, so far as we know," he said. "We'll keep you posted in case our schedules change."

"Sounds good," Lois said.

Lois and Maxwell made their way to the front door then exited the building.

"So what now?" Ethel asked. "Sit here and wait it out or brave the downpour until we get to the car?"

"We could always play another round."

"I just packed everything up."

"Deck of cards?"

"You're on."

* * *

Maxwell and Lois headed toward their vehicle. It was no use. The rain pummeled them and they were thoroughly soaked by the time they got to the car.

Just as Maxwell was about to put the key in the door lock, the whole row of cars shook, setting off car alarms.

"Great," he said. "A downpour *and* an earthquake."

"Get in the car," Lois said.

"Yes, ma'am."

The row of cars shook again as did the others parked across the street.

2

"This is insane," Jordan said.

"Yeah, well, not my fault there was a water break on top of it raining," his supervisor Fitz said. He looked around at the other five guys staring into the sewer. "We got to get down there and fix it up before this whole street goes under water."

"The whole street's gonna go under water anyway because of this damn rain," Jordan said.

"Stop yer complainin' and do your job. Now, first things first. Go down there and assess the damage then radio it back up to me."

It was then Jordan hated the fact their equipment was waterproof. Had it not been, there might have been a slight chance of waiting for the rain to subside before getting to work.

"Fine," Jordan said. He hated his job but it put food on the table for his family of four.

The team lowered Jordan down the sewer hole. Once he hit bottom, he gave the rope a tug to let them know he landed safely. He unclipped his harness from the rope and shone his flashlight into the dark.

"There should be a break somewhere," he said to himself and glanced down at his feet. The water flowed past his boots, which meant he was on lower ground.

Carefully, he made his way forward and then finally found the pipe leading further in the dark.

He radioed to the surface. "You guys shut the water off in this section, yeah?"

"Of course," Fitz said. "See anything?"

"Was just checking and, no, I don't see anything yet."

"Keep looking. We'll send down another guy if we need to."

"Right."

The further he went into the dark and shone the flashlight around, the more he noticed the sewer cavern getting bigger. Somewhere up ahead lay the water break. Somewhere much further up ahead lay a kind of cavern of interconnecting pipes and runoffs.

He used the pipe along the sewer floor as a guide. The sound of gushing water grew louder. Though the water had turned off, there was so much water in the pipes it'd take a good while before they'd run dry.

The ground shook beneath his feet.

"Did you guys feel that tremor?" he said into his radio.

"A little," Fitz said. "The last thing we need is for you to be trapped down there during an earthquake."

"Acknowledged. If it gets too dangerous I'll make my way back."

"Understood."

Jordan kept going until he finally found the break in the line. Water gushed in every direction and got all over him. Thank God for waterproof gear. Still, with so much water spraying this way and that, it was difficult to see anything.

The ground shook again.

He spoke into his radio. "Guys?"

"I know. Another tremor. Find the break?"

"Yep."

"Bad?"

"Yep."

"Okay. We'll let it drain so it's easier to handle. In the meantime start prepping."

"Yeah." Finally, some relief.

A big torrent of water washed over him and sent him sprawling on his back. Then another deluge came down. Jordan coughed up a bit of water.

That was when he shone his flashlight past his feet to see a pair of reptilian eyes staring back at him.

With a scream, Jordan turned the other way and headed straight for his line. He clipped his harness on. "Pull me up! Pull me up!"

"What's going on?" Fitz shouted below.

"Monster. Big monster. Pull me up!"

"Nice try. Get to work. Screw around again and there's going to be disciplinary action."

"I'm serious! Let me up!"

"Stay down there and do your job!"

A low growl, shaking Jordan to the core. Whatever that thing was, it was dangerous. Perhaps even hungry.

"Let me up!" This time his plea for help went unanswered.

The ground shook. Another growl.

Jordan started climbing the rope all the while in disbelief that his boss would ignore his need for help.

His gloves were slick on the rope. The growl grew louder. Screaming, he frantically made his way up the rope only to lose his grip about halfway up. He fell to the sewer ground below.

He looked at his hand. He still had his flashlight. That was what probably made the climbing more difficult. Panic set in and he shone the light down the tunnel. Light reflected off a pair of eyes that reminded him of an alligator, but there was no way an alligator could get into the sewer unless it somehow got in from a runoff drain by the ocean. Even then, the drain was barred off. With a cold shudder, he realized this thing would have had to rip the bars off to get inside.

No animal was that strong, was it?

Those eyes. Dark. Foreboding. So far apart that it couldn't be a gator. His mind wandered and the quick flash that this was some aquatic dinosaur crossed his mind. Before he could shake the thought, the monster scrambled toward him. In the dim light, Jordan couldn't see an end to the thing.

He dropped the flashlight and frantically made his way up the rope only to once again get partway up before something hard and sharp tore through his leg, first one then the other. Howling in pain, he pulled hard on the rope thinking even getting a scant few inches higher might somehow save him.

He pulled and pulled while the thing gnawed at his legs. Then . . . release and this strange sensation of drainage coming from his legs.

One more time. You can do this, he thought. "Help! Help!"

He heard Fitz say, "Oh for crying out loud," and then the sweet yank of salvation as the guys above pulled him up.

"Oh my—" Fitz said.

Jordan looked at his legs. They were torn right off from about mid-thigh down. His femoral artery pumped giant squirt after giant squirt of blood out onto the wet street.

"Gator," was all Jordan could say before everything went dark.

3

George and Ethel had played poker for about an hour when George looked out the window for the umpteenth time.

"It's not getting any better, is it?" Ethel said.

"Nope, and I'm getting tired of poker."

"Wanna play thirty-one?"

"Sorry. I'm carded out."

With a look of disappointment, Ethel said, "Okay," and gave the cards one last shuffle before putting the deck in the box. She got up from the table, presumably to put the cards away.

George stared at the rain. It came down in sheets and they were parked a couple blocks away. They didn't have umbrellas either.

Ethel returned to the table then stared at the window. She glanced back at George and a mischievous grin crossed her face. George knew that grin all too well.

"Why don't we leave, get soaked, go home and take a hot shower together?" she said.

"Oh yeah? And then what?"

She leaned in close and gave him a seductive smile. "Anything you want."

"Ooh." He liked the sound of that, especially since the two of them had been acting like animalistic teenagers and couldn't seem to get enough of each other lately. "Yes," he said, "I think that's a splendid idea."

"Then let's go."

The two stood, pulled on their jackets, and headed toward the door. Once outside, the full force of the rain beat against them and within walking a block, George already felt the water soaking through his jacket.

They passed an alley. Something moved in the dim lighting. Thinking it was just a stray cat or dog, George kept going, but when he heard what sounded like something hard hitting a garbage bin, he had to double back a few steps to see what was what.

"What are you doing?" Ethel said. "Come on."

"Just gimme a sec. Thought I saw something." He went to the mouth of the alleyway. In the first second, his jaw dropped. In the next second, he wet himself.

"George?" Ethel called from some fifteen feet away.

He wanted to say, "Stay there, honey," but the words would not form.

She came by his side. He heard her breathing turn rapid, for there in the alley was an enormous alligator, one bigger than any George had ever seen. He wanted to run. Wanted to hide. Wanted to think this was some kind of practical joke and someone had put a Hollywood prop in there just to scare the daylights out of people. Thing was, it started to move, pulling itself along the ground, slowly at first then faster and faster.

"Run, Ethel," George squeaked. "Ethel?" He glanced beside him. She was gone. He glanced down and there she lay on the pavement, probably having fainted. At least, he hoped she had fainted instead of having had a heart attack.

Suddenly filled with adrenaline, George found himself able to move again. He eyed the creature as he slowly reached down and grabbed his wife by the arm. Carefully but quickly, he dragged her down the sidewalk.

The thing came out of the alley, and in a show of no mercy, propelled itself straight at them. It got to Ethel first and scooped her limp form up into its mouth. With a violent clamping down of its jaws, George watched in horror as the thing began to chew. His wife's bloody arm fell out of the creature's mouth. So did her blood-covered head; it rolled next to his feet. The rain washed the blood away and he could see his wife's beautiful features again.

His chest ached. His heart pounded. A sudden weight settled upon his chest despite standing upright. His left arm went numb and his head began to swoon. No sooner did he realize he was having a heart attack did the giant beast dive at him and pin him to the ground with one foot. As George's head entered its mouth, he thought about his wife, thought about the pain in his chest, thought about crying out for help, thought about the gigantic tooth puncturing his skull.

* * *

Maxwell drove his SUV quickly down the street.

"Come on, slow down," Lois said.

"Not if there's a quake. We need to get out of its way or find somewhere durable enough to survive it."

"Then head home."

"Too far."

"Head. Home."

Knowing not to argue with his wife when she took on that tone, Maxwell pressed the gas pedal further down and hoped there were no cops around to catch him doing it.

The street shook again.

They came upon an intersection, red light pointed toward them. Maxwell slammed on the breaks and both he and Lois lurched forward and pressed again their seatbelts.

Should he run the light? Ah, to heck with it. He checked both ways to make sure the coast was clear then hit the gas and went through.

Something slammed into the side of the vehicle and sent the car tumbling sideways, his world going upside down then right side up then upside down again. The SUV skid to a halt and the ear-piercing screech of the roof scratching along the pavement as it did so set Maxwell's heart racing.

"Lois!"

"I'm here."

The SUV finally came to a stop.

The seatbelt dug into Maxwell's body. He could only assume his wife's did the same to her.

"You . . . you okay?" he asked her.

"I'll live."

Out of his peripheral, Maxwell caught the sight of something huge and dark heading toward them then smashing into the vehicle again, this time sending it skidding up and over a sidewalk curb and crashing it into the side of a building.

Maxwell groaned. So did Lois. Blood ran over his eyes. He looked over at his wife's face. Hers was stained crimson. She must have bounced forward in her seat and smashed her face against the glove compartment before lurching back.

"Lois . . ." he said, barely managing.

She didn't reply.

"Lois," he said more firmly.

Again, she was quiet.

Maxwell groaned again and patted his jacket for his cellphone. He needed to call 911. He couldn't find his phone. It must have fallen from his pocket in the impact.

"Help . . ." he groaned. As if anyone could hear him his voice was so hoarse. He looked to his left and saw the lower half of what looked like a dinosaur coming toward them. The other half was concealed by the rest of the SUV. The thing let go a low guttural growl. He thought he was hallucinating and had hit his head too hard. The thing came closer . . . then another growl, this one coming from the front of the vehicle. He looked forward and couldn't believe his eyes. The alligator was gigantic and had to be some sixty feet long and several feet wide. It was hard to tell in the pouring rain. Its dark eyes bore into him. All he could do was stay there upside down, shaking with fear.

There's another one beside you, he thought. *Don't move. Don't make a sound. Maybe it will go away.*

The gator on the side drove itself forward and smashed into the driver's side of the SUV, sending Maxwell rocking in his seatbelt.

"Lois!" he tried again, this time his voice returning.

The gator's snout got low to the ground and seemed to be sniffing him out. Just then a giant claw tore into Maxwell's chest and ripped him from the vehicle.

4

Lois came to.

"Maxwell?" she said.

Her head hurt. Her face was wet. When she went to touch it then looked at her hand, she saw she was covered in blood. "Maxwell!" He wasn't in the seat beside her.

A low growl.

She looked forward and her breath escaped her when she saw an enormous alligator standing in front of the car. She shook her head to shake herself back to her senses. It hurt like hell. Lois looked to the side. Another one of the creatures, this one even bigger than the one in front of the SUV, had Maxwell pinned under its claws. At first, the thing merely ran its snout up and down the length of Maxwell's body. Then, with lightning speed, shoved its face down into him and bit off the top half of his body.

"Maxwell!" she screamed.

A loud crunch of what she could only assume was bone on metal rocked her to the core. The gator in front had bit into the SUV and began to viciously tear away at it, no doubt to get to the delicious snack within.

Lois scrambled against her seatbelt and tried to find the release button. She found it, pushed it, then hit the roof of the vehicle. Barely able to breathe from the panic, she forced herself to crawl along the roof's interior and make it to the torn-open door on the other side. Giving it everything she had, she pulled herself onto the street.

"Maxwell . . ." she said again.

All that was left of him were a pair of legs on the pavement, which were soon devoured by the monstrosity before her.

The gator that had been at the front of the vehicle moved toward her.

"No, no, nonono," she said and pulled herself to her feet. Her legs were like rubber and she doubted she had the strength to run. She tried anyway and got one step, two steps, three steps, four away from the creature before being plowed back down face-first into the cement. The force of the blow of her forehead hitting the ground echoed throughout her whole body and made stars dance before her vision.

"Get up," she told herself—but she couldn't.

The ground shook beneath her as the thing got closer.

"Oh let me live . . ." she breathed.

Sharp teeth ripped into her back and dug in deep. The gator flung its mouth upward and slowly chomped her down about a foot of her a time. First her feet and shins, then her thighs, then her stomach, then her chest and, finally, her head.

* * *

Paul's insides shook as he watched Emily eat. They'd gone to an old, but incredible, seafood restaurant. Tonight was going to be the night. Oh how he loved her, everything from her jet-black, long hair to her deep brown eyes, to a body that drove him wild from just a mere glance.

She must have caught him jittering because she asked, "Everything okay?"

"Huh? Yeah. Everything's fine." He cracked open a crab leg and got to work on it.

"I know you're a silent eater, but you seem out of sorts," she said.

He brushed his blond hair out of his eyes. "I'm okay. Just a little off tonight." She gave him a wide-eyed expression. "Oh no, don't worry. It has nothing to do with you. It's all me. It's—"

"You're not gonna break up with me, are you?"

"What? Heavens no. No way. Actually" —this was as good a time as any— "Emily" —he got off his chair and got down on one knee before her and produced a small blue jewelry box from his pocket. He opened it and inside was a dazzling engagement ring. "Will you marry me?"

Tears immediately glazed over her eyes and instead of giving him a chance to stand up, she got off her chair and dropped to her knees in front of him. "Oh yes. Most definitely yes." She hugged him then pressed her lips hard against his.

"Really?" Paul looked around. The people in the restaurant had noticed what just happened.

"Yes, dumbass. Of course. I love you so much!"

With the biggest and goofiest smile he could manage, Paul shouted out to the rest of the patrons, "She said yes!"

Claps rose on the air as did the tinkling of cutlery against glasses.

The two got off her knees and took it in. Everyone in the place had a smile on their face. Emily took a curtsey.

"She said yes!" Paul shouted again. He grabbed her and pulled her in fast and tight. He kissed her gently and slid the ring onto her finger.

Heart racing, Paul held Emily's seat out for her and she sat down. He went to the other side of the table and did the same.

As much as he loved lobster and crab, he wasn't sure if the butterflies in his stomach would let him eat.

5

Glancing over at the engagement that just happened, Archie turned his smile into a frown. Here he was with his girlfriend Stacey, and though they had talked marriage, he'd never mustered the guts to finally ask for her hand.

He took a sip of wine. "Hm. Congrats to them."

"Is that a little bitterness I detect?" Stacey said.

"Maybe," he said and popped a garlic and butter shrimp into his mouth.

"Why?"

Now she had him. What was he supposed to say? "That was supposed to be me over there proposing to you"?

"No reason," he said. "Just glad they're in love. Hope they have a happy life."

"I hope so, too." She took a sip of her wine.

They ate in silence for a few minutes before Archie said, "Got that job review next week. I will have been there for a year."

"Is that what's bugging you?"

"In a way."

She furrowed her brow.

"What I mean is, my contract is due for expiration next week hence the review. It's a good job and I don't want to lose it yet there hasn't been any hint from my boss that I've been doing a good job or that there's hope." He worked as an administrator at a high-end cemetery.

"Didn't you say he's pretty quiet, more an" —she made quotes with her fingers— "'observer from the shadows'?"

"That was just the fanboy side of me talking. He's a super nice guy, but hard to read." He took another sip of wine. "All I can do is hope."

Stacey glanced down at her hand. "That's all anyone can do."

They ate in silence for a bit again.

"All's well at your job?" Archie said, searching for something to break the silence. Though he and Stacey endlessly talked all the time, they'd hit patches where communication was minimal.

"It's going fine. Finally got hired on there permanently." She seemed to have caught herself. "Oops. Sorry." She dabbed at her mouth with her napkin.

"It's okay. I love you anyway." He gave her a cheeky grin.

She blushed, which she always did when he poured on the charm. Those beautiful red cheeks of hers. All Archie could do was sigh.

"Well, I'm glad it's going well for you," he said.

She simply nodded then cracked a crab leg open. While she worked at getting the meat out, the floor vibrated and the table began to shake. Archie grabbed hold of it from either side, stabilizing it.

"What the hell was that?" he said.

"Tremors?"

"I don't need another earthquake. The last one was enough and caused enough damage."

"Me neither."

They ate in silence again.

The table shook and the clattering of glasses and plates filled the air. Archie glanced around and saw a lot of others holding onto their tables. One couple had even already got under theirs, and one waiter off to the side purposefully went and stood beneath the doorway that led into the kitchen.

"I think we should go," Archie said.

"I think we should stay," Stacey said.

"We should get to somewhere safe."

"If it is a quake, here is as safe a place as we're gonna be. You don't want to be caught outside if things start tipping over or falling down. Heck, the whole road could go if it's a bad one."

He had to admit she had a point. "You're right. It's best that we stay here."

All seemed to return to normal and nothing shook for a good while until things started up again. This time the table shook so violently that Stacey's plate vibrated over to the edge and fell off.

"My crabs!" She covered her mouth as if ashamed she said something so silly.

The table kept moving and the ground vibrated.

"Under the table," Archie said. "Now!"

They both went under the table and sat right up close to one another. Peering out beneath the table cloth, Archie saw many of the other patrons doing the same, including the couple that just got engaged.

The vibration took on a thunking rhythm. Something wasn't right. Earthquakes didn't pulse.

A quick flash of the famous vibrating water scene from *Jurassic Park* crossed Archie's mind then was gone.

"Archie, what's happening? I'm scared," Stacey said.

He was scared, too, but had to stay strong for her. "I don't know. Just stay put and let's hope it's only a tremor and in a few minutes from now it'll all be—"

An explosion of glass tore through the place; Archie looked out from beneath the table to see a giant green-gray—tail?—swipe through the windows. No. It couldn't be. Not a tail. That was imposs—

The mysterious tail swiped through again, then disappeared.

Heart pounding, he had to shake off Stacey's arm because she was tugging so violently on his it began to hurt.

"What's happening?" she said. "What's happening? Archie, what's happening?"

"I don't know," was all he could say and surely he couldn't tell her what he saw.

"It's the end of the world!" someone—a male—shouted.

"We're all gonna die! The monsters have risen from the earth!" a female screamed.

"Are they right, Archie? Are they?" Stacey said. "What did they mean about monsters? Did they see something? Did *you*?"

"No," he said, hating himself for lying to her.

The booming on the ground increased and a cacophony of screams filled the restaurant. Archie peered out from beneath the tablecloth and could hardly believe his eyes: A giant alligator. Or crocodile. Or something. He always got the two confused. The thing was huge and took up the entire length of the window and then some. Suddenly, it stormed into the restaurant, it's gigantic tail knocking tables up into the air. Some crashed into the walls. Others back where they were. Yet others on top of people, seeming to knock them unconscious.

"What do we do? What do we do?" Stacey asked.

Pray, was all Archie could think. *Pray.*

* * *

Paul held Emily tight as they scrambled to get to the furthest corner of the room away from the giant gator. He pulled her as hard as he could as they made their way across the floor. A splash of blood hit the carpet beside them as growls hit the air behind them.

"Help, Paul, help!" Emily said.

"I'm trying. We need to get as far away from that thing as possible."

They made their way to the farthest side of the room, got into a corner and held onto each other for dear life.

In front of them, the giant gator bit at anything that moved, tearing the heads off some people, tearing others in half. Several were swallowed whole. Some guy off to the side produced a firearm and fired at the thing. The bullets didn't make a dent. The gator stormed over to him and bit him in half, leaving only a pair of legs standing where the guy once stood. The thing's tail tore through the walls and several of the support posts in the restaurant.

"We've got to get out of here before the whole place comes down," Paul said. He took Emily by the hand and said, "Carefully." He pulled her along, ensuring both their backs were to the wall. The entrance was far over to the right. So far, it seemed, the gator was sticking to the main area because that's where the people were.

As they ebbed along the wall, the gator was busy devouring anyone it could. One person it pinned to the floor with its foot then ripped their torso and head apart. Another person it swatted with its tail so that the person went flying against the wall so hard the back of their head blew open, leaving a spatter of blood. The gator crashed its enormous body into the restaurant and knocked away the last standing table. Everyone was without protection.

The door got closer but Paul and Emily still had a good twenty feet or so to go.

"On three, we make a break for it," Paul said.

Emily merely nodded, tears running down her face.

"One. Two. Three."

The two sprinted toward the door.

The gator must have caught sight of them because it immediately headed their way, stepping on people and knocking others over. One person must have seen what Paul and Emily were trying to do so he stood in front of the gator, blocking the monster's path. Lightning quick, the gator tilted its head sideways and bit the man in two, but the diversion was enough to get Paul and Emily out the door.

Once outside, Emily shrieked.

Paul shushed her then felt immediately bad for being so harsh. But this wasn't the time for compassion.

The restaurant sat on a corner and the only part of it safest from the gator was the back alley. Paul and Emily ran toward it only to be greeted by another gator, this one larger than the other.

6

Archie's limbs were rubber and he could only imagine Stacey's were the same. He saw a couple people make a break for the door and made it. He decided he and Stacey should try and do the same.

He gave her a nudge on the shoulder and whispered, "The front door's over there" —he nodded in its direction— "if we—Stacey?"

She sat there shaking, tears running down her face, lower lip quivering.

Archie took her by the shoulders and turned her to face him. "We're going to make a run for the front door, okay? Everything's going to be okay. Do you understand me?"

She didn't respond.

"Do you understand me, Stacey?"

It was near imperceptible but he thought he saw her nod.

"Okay, good," he said, eyes on the door, "then let's go."

When Stacey didn't move, he glanced back at her and she pointed in front of them. The giant gator's face was a mere few feet away.

"So much for that plan," Archie barely managed to whisper.

Stacey screamed at the top of her lungs. The moment the sound hit its highest shrill, the gator lurched forward

and ripped her right from where she sat while also knocking Archie to the side.

"Stacey!" he screamed.

The gator fixated its eyes on him.

Archie thought about how badly he wanted to marry
her. How badly he wanted to wake up next to her each
morning. How badly he wanted romantic nights finished
off with love-making.

But she was gone.

She was go—

The gator lunged for him and swallowed him whole.

* * *

"Quick, turn around!" Paul shouted.

The two did so but the gator was too fast and cut off
the entrance to the alleyway. Emily glanced behind them.
The alley was closed off by another building. They were
trapped and the only possible way out was to somehow
outmaneuver the gator or . . . or . . . there! The fire escape
of the adjacent building.

"Paul," she said then nodded in the direction of the
fire escape.

"Good idea," he said just as the gator growled.

The two made a break for it. When they got beneath
the bottom rung of the ladder leading up to the fire escape,
Emily made a jump for it—and missed. It was too high.

The gator closed in.

"Here," Paul said, cupping his hands. "I'll give you a
boost."

"What about you?"

"No time. Come on. Get on and jump as I push upward."

She placed her foot in his hands.

"On three." The gator growled. "Never mind. On
two."

She nodded her understanding.

The gator was mere feet away.

"One," Paul said, "two." And pushed her upward. She clasped onto the bottom rung of the ladder and started climbing.

Below, the gator bowled over Paul and ate his face.

"Paul!" she screamed.

Then, it was as if she could hear Paul in her head: *Climb. Climb fast.*

Emily tried to ignore the sound of chewing below and she climbed the ladder as fast as she could until she was on the first platform. A few sets of stairs to go and she'd be on the roof and, hopefully, safe. But Paul . . .

The clang and screeching of twisting metal gave her a jolt as the gator stood vertical, trying to get at her.

Legs rubbery, she froze in terror. The thing's mouth was so cavernous it was like an abyss. Its teeth were stained crimson and she saw the top of Paul's head dangling from an enormous tooth.

The gator pulled down on the metal, the jerk enough to make her fall over. She was face to face with it. It snapped at her and narrowly missed her head when she managed to pull herself back.

More metal twisted and contorted . . . then the whole thing came down. Emily rolled off the now vertical platform and down the gator's back, its rough hide digging and cutting into her with each topple. She hit the pavement.

"Getupgetupgetup," she told herself.

She managed to get to her feet and just as soon as she began to run, the gator bit into her legs, crushing them. She fell forward flat on her face, her nose breaking from the sudden impact against the pavement.

Slowly, she was tugged backward as the monster took her in bit by bit, almost as if it wanted her to suffer and wanted to show its power. Once the teeth cut into her middle, she felt a gush of blood leave her body.

Dear God, help me. She knew it was too late and her only hope now was that she would soon be united with Paul in a much better place.

The gator tore into her ribcage and punctured her heart.

7

"Raph would kick Leonardo's butt no problem," Brody said as he and Dustin and Adam stepped their way through the sewer.

"As if," Dustin said. "Leo's their leader. Master Splinter wouldn't have made him leader unless he was the strongest."

"That's horse crap," Adam said. "He made Leo leader because of his smarts."

"No, that's Donnie," Brody said. "He's the genius of the group."

"I meant street smarts, dummy," Adam said.

The three ten-year-old boys stepped through the shallow water inside the sewer. They had found the entrance down near the ocean where the huge runoff pipe looked to have been pried open. They had wanted to get in here for a while and search for the Ninja Turtles after checking out all five flicks. There had to be some modicum of truth to those films. The turtles just looked too real to have been faked.

They each carried a flashlight and shone it this way and that.

"Hello, Mikeeeey," Brody said. "And, by the way, Raph would still hand Leo his head."

"Nuh-uh," Dustin said.

"Then I guess we'll wait and see."

"I guess we will."

They had tied a string to the sewer's entrance and used it as their guide back. The only problem now was the string was running thin on the spool.

"Guys," Adam said. "We're running out of string. I don't want to go any further without it."

"Then this is as far as we go?" Dustin said, disappointment in his voice.

"'Fraid so. Well, maybe six feet further then we're out."

"Gah!" Brody said. "We should have brought double that. Even triple. Just tie the ends together and this whole place could be our ticket for finding the Tur—"

A growl echoed throughout the chamber.

"Did you hear that?" Dustin whispered.

"Yeah," Adam said, fear already in his voice.

"Turtles don't growl," Brody said.

"What sound do they make, anyway?" Dustin asked.

"Beats me. Regular turtles are so slow and stupid and just sit there. The Ninja Turtles can talk."

There was that low rumble again.

"Guys, I don't like the sound of it," Adam said.

"Me neither," Brody said.

"You guys are a bunch of wusses," Dustin said.

Another growl, this one louder and getting closer.

"I'm heading back," Adam said.

"Me, too," Brody added.

"Well, I can't keep going alone," Dustin said.

All three of them shone their flashlights ahead. Dustin thought he saw movement but could have been mistaken.

"Screw this, I'm done," Adam said.

"Me, too," Brody said. "We can research turtle sightings on-line or something."

Dustin sighed. "Fine."

Adam started winding up the string as the three made their way back.

Another growl, this one even closer.

Adam frantically started winding the string while the two others walked quickly beside him.

This time the growl sounded like it was right behind them. Dustin looked but didn't see anything. "Grab the string in bunches instead of winding it so tight. It'll be faster."

"Then it'll get all tangled," Adam said.

"Doesn't matter right now," Dustin said. "Something's behind us."

"Bunch it," Brody said and Dustin chuckled. It had sounded like he said, "Punch it," as in move faster.

Adam worked as quickly as he could. The three boys wound left then right then left then right, then went straight, then turned again—all following the string.

A circle of light appeared before them. The entrance to the sewer.

"Phew, we made it," Adam said.

There was another growl, this one causing the sewer walls and floor to vibrate. Then thudding as if something huge stomped its way toward them.

"Move!" Adam said, and the three sprinted for the opening.

Dustin tripped and landed face-first in the water.

"Dustin!" Brody said and doubled back to help his friend up.

Just as Brody got Dustin to his feet, that's when they saw it, and it was no Ninja Turtle.

They shrieked and ran for the opening before diving out into the ocean. Dustin quickly made his way ashore. The moment Dustin's feet touched the rocks, a giant splash hit the water. He looked at his friends and they swam toward him.

Then the thing surfaced, most of its body submerged under water, but it didn't matter. The water was still clear enough coming off the runoff drain that Dustin knew what he was looking at: a giant alligator, the biggest he'd ever seen.

The gator went under the water and the next thing Dustin knew, Adam had been pulled under, the only sign of him having been in the water a floating pool of blood.

"No!" Dustin shouted.

"Help me," Brody said. "I'm not a good swimmer."

Dustin's legs shook from fear.

"Don't just stare at me. Come get me!"

"I-I . . ."

The gator surfaced beside Brody and ate him in one bite.

Tears poured down Dustin's face and he screamed so loud his voice went hoarse.

The gator swam toward him and was on the rocks faster than Dustin expected. He turned to run but the best he could manage was a feeble hobble he was so scared.

The rocky ground thudded, then stopped, then an enormous weight landed on Dustin and he felt the front of his body slowly peel apart as the monster squished him.

8

The downpour ended shortly before the next evening. Pulled off to the side of the road in mid downtown, Officer Morris May sat in his squad car, digging into a bag of donuts. He always ordered three. He told himself it was because of his three kids and he was having one for each of them. It was a bullcrap excuse. The real problem was he enjoyed donuts a little too much. Even his doctor said getting three daily would eventually cause him some trouble.

He patted his stomach. Yep. Chubby as ever. He'd have to do something to control the weight, but these donuts were just too damn good and, yes, he knew he was playing into a stereotype: Cops and their donuts.

He took a sip of coffee, set the cup back down in its holder, then wondered what his wife Veronica was making for dinner that night. Hopefully steak. There was nothing like a good barbecued steak to satisfy the soul. Unfortunately, he was not a grill master so his wife worked the barbecue while he'd eagerly wait at the dinner table with his beer, counting down the seconds until she brought it to him.

A low rumble vibrated throughout the vehicle. Then it stopped. Like any good Los Angeles resident, he thought it might be an earthquake starting up. He hated earthquakes, and while the destruction they wrought was awful and often tragic, he didn't like how it made his stomach all woozy as the roads vibrated and sometimes moved.

He chomped down on his strawberry jelly-filled donut. As he chewed, another tremor went through the police car.

"Great," he said. "Here I am out in the open." He wished he was on desk duty today. If he was and an earthquake took place, there were plenty of places in the precinct to hide. Out here in his car, well, all he had was the car.

Up at the crossroads ahead, screaming people began to run past.

"What the—" he said.

Cars ripped down the cross street, clearly zipping over the speed limit.

"Here we go," Morris said and adjusted his seatbelt.

He put the car in gear, flicked on the sirens, and headed straight toward the commotion. There were too many cars whipping by and too many people crossing the road that he couldn't get a good look at what was happening. He got out of the vehicle and went amongst the screaming people on foot. He looked to the left and there was nothing out of the ordinary other than the speeding cars. He pressed his lips together knowing there was no way he'd be able to ticket each one.

He looked to the right and didn't see anything either other than the craziness. Some people bumped into him as they ran past.

"Everybody calm down," he shouted. No one did and they kept running.

He looked left again. Just those speeding cars. He looked right and . . . and—

"What the hell?" he said.

Around a hundred feet away was this dark gray-green mound thrashing about.

It was coming closer.

He started to weave his way in between the people to try and get a closer look.

Then he saw it.

A giant alligator over three car lengths long. The creature bit and chewed up as many people as it could as they crossed its path.

A final vehicle sped by.

Hands shaking, breathing becoming choppy, Morris felt his shoulder for his radio. Crap. He left the damn thing in the car. As fast as he could, he ran back to his vehicle and by the time he collapsed in his seat, he was out of breath. He picked up the radio.

"This is May. We got a Code . . . um . . . Code . . ." What code was there for a giant alligator? "I'm at sixth and seventh. We got a . . . giant alligator tearing down the street. It's, um, it's eating people and destroying property. I need backup. Call pest control or animal control or whoever is in charge of animal clean up in this city."

"Ha ha, very funny, May," the voice came over the speaker. "Repeat what you said again so all of us here at dispatch can hear you."

"I said we got a giant alligator coming down the street at sixth and seventh. It's like Godzilla but not as big." He heard the laughter on the other end.

"This channel is for serious business only, May. Stop screwing around."

"I'm not, I swear! Put my job on the line. I'll turn in my badge if you don't believe me. Get a chopper up in the air and they'll see exactly what I'm seeing."

"Sorry, no go. Stop the BS and do your job."

"Please, I beg you. Send down another car. Send a helicopter up in the air. If I'm lying, screw turning my badge in. Let Captain Ordoway fire me. I swear I'm telling the truth."

The sigh on the other end was big and loud.

The cop car rocked a little side to side as the thing down the street no doubt got closer.

"Fine. We'll send up a chopper."

"Thank you. Thank you. Thank you. I'll try and tail the thing and keep you guys posted."

"Whatever you say, Officer Gator."

The people had cleared the area. Morris put the car in drive and crept up to the intersection. The enormous alligator was not far off, a mere twenty feet. What was he supposed to do? Shoot it?

"It's all I can do," he said and slowly opened the driver's side door. The gator was a mere ten feet away. Morris produced his sidearm and hoped to God he didn't anger the thing and it'd come after him.

He fired a single shot. The bullet hit the gator in the side, but the thing kept moving.

He fired again and the gator turned its attention on him. Panic setting in with a million lumps in his throat, Morris fired shot after shot until he was out of ammo. He got back into the police car, searching for more. Then the vehicle tipped forward and he hit his head on the steering wheel. Giving his head a quick shake, he looked out the windshield. The gator had one scaly foot on the hood of the car and, just behind it, its gigantic head with dark eyes staring at him.

There's no way it's that smart, Morris thought.

Freaking out, he shouted, "There's no way you're that smart!" And slammed the car into drive and hit the gas as hard as he could. The vehicle lunged forward, nailing the creature. But the thing didn't budge from its position. It was just way too heavy and took the impact no problem.

A big set of jaws opened wide.

Morris's eyes opened even wider, so much so he thought his eyeballs would roll out of his head.

The gator plowed its face into the windshield, shattering the glass and bending the metal of the roof backward like a sardine can.

"Oh shi—" The gator's face lunged forward again and its front teeth grabbed Morris by the middle and pulled him straight from the car.

Morris felt the heat of blood run down his legs. The thing tossed him up into the air and readjusted its bite, biting into his torso even further. Blood spurted out on either side of Morris's peripheral, the pain from the bite unbearable.

Suddenly, all his muscles went limp while the thing chewed him alive.

The last thing Morris heard was the sound of a chopper up overhead.

9

The gator made its way through the sewer system and back to the runoff drain. It climbed over the bars it had destroyed earlier and splashed into the ocean.

It was still hungry.

* * *

The beach was starting to empty of swimmers as the evening wore on. Today, Shelley had taken the day off work for some R and R and swimming was at the top of her list.

She swam through the water, having spent the better part of the day in the ocean instead of on land. Her shoulders burned though and she knew she'd have a wicked sunburn after today. She paused and treaded water, looking at the sand some forty meters away. The lifeguards were still on duty, each decked out in red swimwear as if this beach could dub as a location for a *Baywatch* episode.

She stopped treading and moved through the water again. She didn't have plans of leaving anytime soon.

Ten minutes later after a round of straight swimming, she treaded water again. As she did, she felt something rough brush against the bottom of her feet. She instinctively pulled her knees up so her feet could avoid whatever it was.

After catching her breath, she swam a little more then fatigue hit her full force and she decided to make her way inland and take a break sitting on the sand. As she swam through the water, that same rough thing brushed under her entire body.

"Ow," she said absentmindedly. *What was that thing?* Then she froze. What if it had been a shark and its fin that scratched along the length of her body? Should she call out for help? Should she run up to the lifeguards on duty and tell them there was a shark in the water?

She picked up her pace, swimming one arm over the other until something grabbed her by the leg and pulled her under the water. It took her down, down, down.

This was no shark.

A quick mental flash of it being a Kraken crossed her mind but she didn't feel any tentacles. Silly. Panic seizing her, she swam against the thing and felt this giant body that was ridged on what she assumed was its underside. She pushed against it but to no avail. She hammered at it with her fists with no luck. Her lungs hurt from the little held breath.

Then the thing released her and she frantically swam back to the surface. Once she broke the water, she took in a huge lungful of air.

"Hey!" She coughed. "Help!" She waved her arms in the direction of the lifeguards. Some were busy talking and the guy on the high lookout chair was looking the other way.

"Help! Help me!" Shelley yelled.

Finally, the guy's attention focused on her.

"Help!"

Immediately he was in action and climbed down the lookout and blew his whistle, springing the others to attention. Three of them ran toward her.

That rough thing ran under her body again and once more went for her legs. This time it bit into them. Shelley shrieked from the pain and saw red water floating around her.

"Help!" she said, reaching out her hand.

Whatever this thing was, it had her and wouldn't let go. It pulled on her legs and then as if it was on purpose, slowly tore her legs off from just over the knee downward. She screeched in pain. Having only her arms to rely on, she swam toward the lifeguard. She was almost there. *He* was almost there. She reached out and he first took hold of her fingers and then her whole hand and brought her into himself. He must've seen the bloody water because he blew his whistle again.

"Shark!" he shouted at his comrades. They got into action and one ran back to the viewing deck, went inside, then came out with a bullhorn.

Barely conscious, Shelley heard, "Everyone out of the water now! I repeat, everyone out of the water now!"

She lost consciousness for a moment then awoke as the lifeguard pulled her onto shore. Shelley looked down at her legs and the sight of the torn flesh made her pass out again.

* * *

Ray looked at the woman at his feet. It had to have been a shark. Possibly two of them. Her legs were a mess of ropey flesh and blood that stained the sand. He glanced out onto the water, looking for fins. He didn't see any.

"Get out of the water! I repeat, get out of the water!" came Heather's voice over the bullhorn.

People started making their way toward shore and exiting the ocean. They stood around murmuring amongst themselves, no doubt discussing what could be wrong.

Heather ran up to Ray. "Oh my," she said. "What happened?"

"I don't know. I don't—"

An enormous green-gray body emerged from the water and crawled its way up on the sand. It was an alligator. A gigantic alligator.

Ray's breath quickened and he heard Heather's do the same. People started screaming and running further up the beach, even onto the grass that led to the parking lot beyond.

Ray grabbed the woman on the ground and threw her over his shoulder. He and Heather made a break for it.

"Just run," he said.

The ground vibrated beneath his feet. He tripped onto the sand, taking the woman over his shoulder with him.

"Ray!" Heather said and came over. She rolled the woman off him and helped him up. Without wasting a moment, he once again threw the woman over his shoulder and ran with Heather further from the water.

The ground still vibrated.

"Ray!" Heather yelled.

He glanced over his shoulder; the creature had caught up to Heather and was on top of her. It pitched its enormous head downward and gnawed at Heather's face.

"Run. Just run," he told himself. He didn't know if the woman he carried was dead or alive. Right now it didn't matter. He'd find out soon enough once he got them to safety.

Quickly, the woman was jerked from his grip. He looked over his shoulder again; the gator worked its way up her body, swallowing her one chunk at a time.

Legs turning to noodles, he kept running but the thing behind him wouldn't have it and kept on his tail. He'd never seen a live alligator in his life, never mind one so big. Did they always grow that big or was this some freak occurrence? He didn't know. All he knew was he had to run.

It wasn't long before teeth nipped at his ankles. It was mere seconds after that the gator's giant body rolled over him like a tank over a car. He couldn't move and couldn't breathe. The thing's weight pressed him against the sand. Try as he might to create some sort of movement, nothing happened. It was just too heavy.

A violent sting ripped through his back and then multiple sharp punctures worked their way into the open wound.

It would be seconds before it got to his heart.

God have mercy on me, he thought.

Seconds before his heart.
Seconds before his heart.
Seconds before his he—

10

Jimmy headed with the chopper to sixth and seventh. His co-pilot, Steve, sat with his arms crossed while Jimmy worked the controls. He could tell by Steve's body language that he wasn't impressed. Morris was known for his practical jokes and concocting some story about giant alligators, well, he wouldn't put it past him.

As they flew, Jimmy thought of what he'd do to Morris if this whole thing turned out to be bunk. Then he thought, what if Morris was right? What if there was a giant alligator terrorizing the city?

Nah, he thought.

They were soon over sixth and seventh. Jimmy brought the chopper down low enough so Steve and he could get a clear visual as to what was happening on the ground. As they descended, Jimmy caught sight of a new chopper flying toward the scene as well. Unless Morris went way overboard and phoned in a hoax, there would have to be some truth to his claim. Jimmy's heart sped up at the possibility.

He noticed Steve uncross his arms and peer out the window. Then Steve gave him a whack on the shoulder.

"Look," Steve said.

Jimmy looked out his side of the glass, and there, below, was an enormous gator making its way through the streets.

Immediately, Jimmy reached for the radio but Steve already had it in hand.

"Report: giant alligator walking the street. Repeat, giant alliga—correction, there are now two of them," Steve said.

"Report confirmed," came the voice through the radio. "It's all over the TV."

"Two gators," Jimmy said to himself. He looked out the window again. Now there weren't two. There were three. How many of these things were there?

"Send animal control," Steve said, his voice wavering. "Sent pest control. Send damn monster control. I don't know what you call it but send someone."

"Roger. Heard and understood," the radio voice said.

Steve looked over at Jimmy. "Damn." He drew out the word. "Morris was right." He looked out the window. "I don't see his car."

"Let's hope he's all right," Jimmy said. "As for us, I can't land us here so we're turning around and . . . and . . . coming back in a squad car with the biggest weapons we've got."

* * *

Jimmy and Steve returned to the scene with an entourage of cop cars. He knew, like himself, the other officers were decked out in protective gear, especially the SWAT team.

They pulled up and slowly got out of their vehicles, shotguns drawn, armed and ready. Other cars joined up beside them and were parked as such to let the large SWAT vehicle through. The moment the SWAT vehicle stopped, a pile of men came out, each armed with standard weaponry plus a shotgun of their own.

The police cars formed a semi-circle around the gators. Jimmy made his way to the front of the line where Captain Pierce just stood there with a look of disbelief on his face.

"Captain, what do we do?" Jimmy asked.

Pierce slowly shook his head. "I don't know. I mean, I do know, but there ain't exactly anything in the rule book about this. I think we have no choice but to simply open fire and put these things down."

Jimmy nodded then went back behind his open police door and waited for the order. When it was given, every cop blasted their shotguns at the creatures, the bullets striking their thick hides. Instead of killing them, the gators fully turned in their direction and started moving toward them.

"Keep firing!" Pierce shouted through his bullhorn.

The bullets kept on, but they didn't seem to faze the gators.

SWAT members threw out a couple of grenades and the explosions rocked the neighborhood, sending up a cloud of dust and smoke. For a second, Jimmy thought they got the animals but soon they emerged from the smoke and began to pick up speed.

"Ah sh—" Jimmy said before Pierce shouted through the bullhorn, "Keep at 'em. They'll have to break down at some point." Judging by the tone of Pierce's voice, Jimmy thought he didn't sound too convincing.

The gators stomped right up to the police barricade with their mouths open.

Jimmy froze and it was as if all that he'd seen before had finally caught up with him.

Monstrous gators.

Three of them.

All pointed their way and coming in fast. He knew from watching *Swamp People* that gators could move fast on land. He could only imagine how fast these ones could move if they fully put on the steam.

The cops kept firing. The gators kept coming. Those hides of theirs—they could very well be bulletproof.

One gator came in and devoured three SWAT members in one go. Jimmy caught the guy's eyes pleading for help before he was swallowed.

Another gator changed its direction then came in from the side and took out a pair of cops. Blood sprayed from its mouth when it chomped down on them like a couple packets of ketchup.

The smallest gator came straight for Jimmy. In his panic, he knew what he was seeing but his brain couldn't wrap itself around it.

"Look out," someone said and shoved Jimmy out of the way just as the gator's mouth clamped shut around him.

Laying there on the pavement, reality reset itself and Jimmy came back to the present. He got up on shaky legs and saw the carnage around him. Blood-covered cop cars with miscellaneous body parts littered the scene. The small gator came in and tried again for Jimmy. He ran out of the way in a fresh surge of adrenaline; the gator's head smashed into the side of the cop car.

Screams and shouts filled the air and the three gators worked to devour the humans.

"Jimmy," Captain Pierce said. Jimmy put his eyes in his direction. The medium-sized gator had his captain in its mouth. "Help."

Pierce reached out with both hands. Jimmy ran over, firing at the beast to no avail, then re-holstered his weapon and grabbed Pierce's blood-slicked hands. Jimmy pulled but the blood made it impossible for their hands to remain connected. Jimmy fell backward and hit the ground, whacking his tailbone.

"Argh," he said. Damn did that hurt.

He got up and went back to his captain and this time gripped him by the forearms. He pulled and pulled.

"Pull," Pierce said.

"I'm trying. I'm—" Jimmy fell backward again when Pierce's arms let loose from his body. The last Jimmy saw of him was his head being crushed between enormous teeth. It took a moment, then Jimmy realized he still held onto Pierce's arms. He dropped them and took a step back.

SWAT members were in the gators' mouths as were the remaining men and women in uniform.

He was the last one left. He had no choice but to run. Just as he turned heel, a low growl grew louder behind him.

Jimmy put on the speed as best he could then was suddenly tossed up into the air. He flipped over and fell face-first into the cavernous mouth of a giant alligator.

Captain Christine Nightengale of the US Army couldn't believe what she was hearing over the radio. Allegedly, there were three giant alligators slaughtering people on the streets of LA. Surely this had to be a joke—yet if it was—why be called to the scene? It could be a test, even if a really dumb one: What kind of emergency should one respond to?

She kept an eye on the Jeep's radio, waiting for the next report. It wasn't long until the radio came to life.

"We have visual confirmation. Three enormous alligators making their way through the city streets, devouring everything in their path. Local police have been lost to the creatures. Over."

She glanced at Kyle, a sergeant, who rode in the passenger seat.

"I can't believe this. This is ridiculous," he said. He then pointed to the radio. "But there you have it, plain as day."

Christine wondered why they didn't bomb the damn things and could only imagine avoiding property damage and accidental civilian death were the reasons.

She kept driving. Other Jeeps followed behind as did a tank. Overhead, the echoing boom of jets filled her ears. Their fly-bys must have been what confirmed the sighting. Unfortunately, their wingspan and sheer power eliminated any chance of them flying low and taking out the creatures with their own weaponry.

According to the Jeep's GPS, they were almost there. Christine braced herself for what she might see. She noticed Kyle grip his seat's armrest and guessed he was probably doing the same.

She slowed as she rolled up to the GPS's coordinates then put the brakes on completely.

There was nothing here. Nothing but an empty street and—The ground rumbled. She looked at Kyle. His eyes were wide. They both produced their AR-15s and proceeded further forward from the vehicle. The opening and closing of doors behind her told her the other soldiers were doing the same except for the boys in the tank. They would stay put and await further orders.

Guns raised, she and Kyle and the others slowly made their way down the street.

The ground vibrated again.

Despite her training to stay calm in a crisis, Christine's heart began to pick up speed.

The street was still empty. Had they got the coordinates wrong? The army wouldn't make such a stupid mistake. But if these supposed gators were on the move, then it would make sense the coordinates would change.

The ground shook again.

And that's when she saw it: a giant alligator. She could hardly believe her eyes . . . but there it was.

"Open fire?" Kyle said.

"Open fire."

Christine took her shots and let the AR-15 run rampant. She heard Kyle beside her do the same. The bullets struck the beast and drew its attention. It lunged itself forward. Christine and Kyle both dove away in opposite directions as the creature crashed in between the Jeeps.

Christine looked back over her shoulder and saw the alligator devour two soldiers: one by tearing off the top half of their body; the second by going for the legs and ripping the soldier in half.

She kept her aim and kept firing. Then it hit her: blind the damn thing.

"Go for the eyes," she told Kyle. He nodded his understanding.

Christine aligned her shot and opened fire. The bullets hit the gator directly in the eye. Where the eye once was was now a smattering of torn flesh and blood. The thing thrashed about and Christine assumed Kyle had hit his mark as well. The creature's giant tail slammed into the Jeeps, knocking them over sideways. One Jeep landed on a soldier and before Christine could get to their aid, the soldier, probably out of panic, blew his own brains out.

The cranking of metal filled her ears and she noticed the tank aim its cannon at the beast. It opened fire and blew a hole into the thing's neck. Blood sprayed out like a guiser. The thing spun around as if trying to escape. The tank let it have it again, this time blowing a hole in its middle. Finally, the thing stopped moving.

With a smile that quickly turned into a frown, Christine looked at the damage wrought.

One down, two to go.

12

Christine and Kyle quickly scrambled to the last remaining Jeep and fired it up.

"Where are the other two," Kyle asked.

"Dunno. Should be around here somewhere."

"That was freak luck back there, wasn't it?"

"Luck, a good shot, call it what you want." She glanced in the rearview mirror and saw the tank following them.

She came up to an intersection and looked left then right. On the right side, the other two gators stood there as if waiting for something.

Christine guided the Jeep up and over the curb onto the sidewalk.

"Same plan," she told Kyle.

"That was actually a plan back there?"

"You know what I mean."

They both exited the Jeep, guns ready.

The tank rolled slowly behind Kyle as he acted as their eyes and ears to the outside world. They turned a corner and one of the giant gators tossed a civilian into the air and chomped down on them.

"I have visual," Kyle radioed into the tank.

The tank's hatch opened and a soldier popped their head out. He shouted something to his comrades within but Kyle couldn't quite make it out. He checked around for Christine and wanted to make sure she was safe. He cared for her, deeply, but now wasn't the time to dwell on it.

The gator caught sight of them and started its approach. Kyle and Christine fired a steady stream of bullets at the thing, but it kept advancing.

"I'm blinding it," she said and set up her shot. When the bullets hit, the creature roared and barreled toward Kyle, catching him in its jaws.

"No!" Christine shouted.

"Fire!" Kyle said into his radio, wanting the boys in the tank to take their shot.

The creature's teeth mashed down into Kyle's middle, squirting out his intestines.

The last thing he heard was the echoing boom of the tank taking its shot.

* * *

Christine screamed and shouted, "You bastard!" She sent a barrage of bullets at the creature even though the shot from the tank blew its head off, taking Kyle along with it.

"Where's the other one? Where's—" There was a low growl behind her. She turned, and just on the other side of the tank was the last gator.

"Get into position," she shouted into her radio.

"Understood."

While the tank maneuvered itself, Christine let the final gator have it and fired shot after shot until her gun ran dry. She reloaded and kept firing. The creature sprang at her; she jumped back. It sprang at her again and clipped her arm with its powerful jaws.

She glanced over her shoulder. The tank was in position.

She went to move out of the way so it could fire but the beast grabbed her by the arm and with each chew slowly drew her into its mouth. The last sound she heard before the beast bit into her head was the defeaning blast of the cannon firing.

EPILOGUE

Deep within the sewer was a nest of alligator eggs.
Some were open.

About the Author

A.P. Fuchs is the author of many novels and short stories. His most recent efforts of putting pen to paper are *Axiom-man/Auroraman: Frozen Storm; Flash Attack: Thrilling Stories of Terror, Adventure, and Intrigue;* and *Axiom-man Episode No. 3: Rumblings.*

Also a cartoonist, he is known for his superhero series, *The Axiom-man Saga,* both in novel and comic book format.

Fuchs's main website is
www.canisterx.com

Join his free weekly newsletter at
www.tinyletter.com/apfuchs

* 9 7 8 1 9 2 7 3 3 9 7 3 2 *